Blood Stains From the Past

Blood Stains From the Past

P J   W R I G H T

authorHOUSE®

AuthorHouse™ LLC
1663 Liberty Drive
Bloomington, IN 47403
www.authorhouse.com
Phone: 1-800-839-8640

Published by AuthorHouse   10/08/2013

ISBN: 978-1-4918-2731-4 (sc)
ISBN: 978-1-4918-2730-7 (e)

Library of Congress Control Number: 2013918215

CHAPTER 1

 s Ashlie stared out the cabin window large fluffy snow flakes fell to the already snow covered ground. She shivered at the sight of the snow. Just two days ago she was sitting on the balcony enjoying the sun. She had to get away. She thought she had put her past behind her. But five days ago it came back to haunt her. First it was a phone call, and then it was letters in her mail box. They said they knew what she was hiding and they were going to ruin her life. She planned on staying and fighting back. But it was no use. She was too exhausted and stressed out. She had to get away. She called in and said she was using her vacation. She'd be back in a couple of weeks. She figured that would give her enough time to work it out and I guess if she couldn't work it out she would disappear into the woodwork. If her past was ever exposed she knew she would have to.

Ashlie worked her butt off to be where she was today and she wasn't about to let some lunatic take it away from her. She wrapped her hand around her cup of hot cocoa and just stared out the window, she was so lost in thought that she hadn't realized how much snow had fallen. She turned around and went and sat down in the chair next to the fireplace. She pulled a blanket up around her and stared into the flames of the fire she had built earlier. She dozed off to sleep. She started dreaming; she was a little girl and she was playing in the snow with her sister. They were having fun playing fox and the goose. She was chasing her sister and they were laughing, then she hears a voice yelling for her to get in the house. She doesn't want to go. She knows what's going to happen. She looks at her sister and starts crying. The voice gets louder. She starts yelling NO! NO MORE! Ashlie wakes up in a cold sweat. The nightmares were starting again.

Ashlie had poured everything she had into her career as a police detective. She started out as a police office. She went to night school and studied real hard to get her detective badge. The harder she worked the less she thought about her past. When she was born her mother wanted a son. She went off the deep end when Ashlie was born. She couldn't accept that she had another girl. She wouldn't hold her or even look at her. She got worse when the doctors told her that she couldn't have anymore kids. So she decided to make Ashlie a boy. She dressed her like a boy. She told people that her baby's name was Ashton. When she started potty training her she made her stand up. When she would pee down her legs, she would endure terrible beatings at the hands of her mother. The girls would taunt her in gym class. She would go off by herself to get dressed. One day a bunch of girls got together and dragged her into the shower and held her down and dump shampoo all over her. Ashlie had to be careful how she acted around her mother. Her father left. She couldn't blame him. She just wished he would have taken her with him. Everyone understood that she was a girl except her mother. One day when Ashlie was about fifteen, she was getting another one of her mother's beating, Ashlie snapped and the last thing she remembered is waking up and sitting next to her mother with a large butcher knife in her hand. Then her sister Dee was standing there and Ashlie was holding her mother. Dee called the cops. Ashlie was released into her sister's custody. The doctors said she was driven to kill her mother. Their secret had been kept hidden until now. Ashlie wish she could remember what happened. She only knows what Dee told her. Ashlie knew she would loose her career if it got out she had killed her mother. She had never told anyone that on that day, she felt as though both her and her mother had been set free.

When Ashlie woke up the sun was setting. She got up to fix her something to eat. She really didn't feel like eating, but her stomach was growling. She fixed herself a ham and cheese sandwich. That seemed to hit the spot. She cleaned up the kitchen and went in and turned on the TV in the dining room. The news was on. Ashlie wished she hadn't turned it on. The newscaster just announced another brutal murder had occurred. Another man had been found, his personals had been removed just like the others. Man, Ashlie said to herself, that is one angry person. I wonder what they do with the parts when they cut them off. When she left for her vacation they hadn't determined yet if the men were already dead when they were butchered. It made all the men in the department cringe thinking about it. Ashlie was having fun teasing them about it. I suppose they'll be calling me back to work. I better turn in early. Ashlie got up and headed for bed. She hoped that she wouldn't have any nightmares tonight. She needed her sleep. And she wasn't getting very much of it lately. It wasn't long after her head hit the pillow and she was out. She started dreaming about her partner Skyler. They were in her bedroom and he was kissing her. He started unbuttoning her shirt, then he slipped his hand into her shirt. Ashlie was getting really turned on. What a dream she thought to herself. She'd always had a crush on her partner, but she was afraid to pursue it. She was afraid he didn't feel the same way and he would laugh at her. So she kept it to herself. Ashlie was sound asleep when the phone rang. She jumped straight up in bed. She was afraid to pick up the receiver. Reluctantly she picked it up and said,

"Hello."

"Ashlie, is that you?" asked Skyler.

"No, it's the Easter Bunny," said Ashlie, sarcastically.

"Very funny Ashlie," he said. "The reason I'm calling, is because there was another murder and we need you here ASAP."

"I had a feeling you guys might call," she said, "I was watching the news."

"So how fast can you get here?" he asked.

"Can I get dressed and pack my things, first?" she said.

"Sure no problem, I'll let them know your coming," he said.

"Sure no problem," she said.

"Okay, goodbye," said Skyler. "Before I hang up, I just wanted to say thanks."

"Sure," Ashlie said.

As she hung up the phone she said to herself, I wish he was calling to say he missed me and wanted to make mad passionate love to me. Ashlie decided to take a quick shower to wake her up. She had a three hour drive ahead of her. After her shower she felt refreshed. She hurried and got dressed. She packed her suit case and left her key to the cabin on the table. She already called the office and told them she was checking out. She paid with a credit card so she didn't have to sign anything. She carried her bags out to the car. She put them in the trunk, closed the lid and got in the car. She put the key in the ignition. She was in such a hurry that she hadn't noticed the windshield was covered in snow. She started the car and got out and cleaned off the windshield. The snow had stopped falling sometime ago. Ashlie was glad, because it will make it easier to see the road on the way home, she thought to herself. She put the car in reverse and backed around, then she put in low and headed slowly down the road. Ashlie notice that all the other cabins were dark, except one. The lights were on. They sure are up early Ashlie thought to herself. As her headlights shined on the trees she could see the snow had weighed down the branches. It seemed as though they were giant catapults getting ready to launch. The snow glittered like diamonds on the ground as her lights shown on the ground. It seemed like forever before she reached the main road. The snow plows had been out and cleared the road. But she could tell the roads were icy. She putted along 25 mph. She didn't want to go off the road. This is going to be a long trip home, she said to herself. She turned on her radio. Several cars flew by Ashlie throwing snow and slush over her windshield. She'd curse them as she turned her wipers on to clean it. Don't expect me to stop if you end up in the ditch she'd yell. Like they can her me she'd say to herself. As she slowly made her way down the road she came up on a couple of vehicles that had went past her and slid off the road. She laughed and waved as she passed them by. The highway patrol was there helping them get out. The sun was starting to come up over the mountains. Ashlie was glad to see it. She was never to keen about driving in the snow at night. She spotted a sign that said, gas and eats 2 miles. Good, said Ashlie, I'm starving. Fifteen minutes later Ashlie pulled into the restaurant. It seemed like she had been driving for hours. It felt good to get out and stretch her legs.

Ashlie remembered passing up the restaurant on the way up to the cabin, but she didn't stop. When she walked in the door she could see that it was pretty busy. The waitresses were really hopping. Finally someone came over and asked her if she wanted smoking or nonsmoking. Ashlie usually preferred nonsmoking, but she was so hungry that she told the waitress that she didn't care. And wouldn't you know it, she put her right next to a couple that was lighting them up as fast as they put them down. The smell about made Ashlie gag. Ashlie wished she had said nonsmoking. As she picked up the menu to look at it a cockroach ran across the table. Ashlie jumped. She got up and headed for the door. She decided she would get a box of donuts at the gas station. The waitress looked at her funny as she headed for the door. It didn't bother her to look at murder victim. But she wasn't about to share breakfast with a large bug. She figured the service probably sucked anyways. She pulled into the gas station and about choked when she saw the price of gas, $4.15 a gallon. If it wasn't for the fact that she was down to a ¼ of a tank, she would have kept going. She didn't even want to think about how much that box of donuts was going to cost. When Ashlie got out to the car she opened the box and took out a donut and slowly ate it. She savored every bite. She wasn't going to hurry it, because at $4.00 a box she was going to enjoy every bite and every donut.

Ashlie pulled out onto the road and headed for home. She knew they would be chomping at the bit. From the very first murder, this case had been her baby. She study it forward and backward. She had come up with several theories, but none of them seem to pan out. But she wasn't giving up. Who ever it was, for some reason or another, their target was men. When Ashlie drove to the bottom of the canyon road she was over looking the City. It was kind of good to almost be home she thought to herself. Ashlie was so busy trying to figure out the case, that the trip seemed to go fast. She wasn't to far from her apartment. She loved her place, because it over looked the Zoo. She loved going there on her days off. As she passed it she noticed the ambulance there. Someone must've got hurt feeding the animals she said to herself. She pulled into the car port and turned her car off. She sat there for a minute. She knew that once she was in her apartment she wouldn't have a moments rest. She got out and opened the trunk and took out her bags. As she was heading up the stairs an elderly neighbor stuck her head out the door and called to Ashlie. Ashlie turned around and went back down to the stairs.

"Yes, what is it, Mrs. Day?" asked Ashlie.

"The mailman left you a package while you were gone," she said.

She hands Ashlie the package.

"Thank you," said Ashlie.

"I thought I'd better keep it for you, beings no one knew how long you were going to be gone," she said.

"That was very thoughtful of you," said Ashlie.

"It came this morning, I noticed there was no return address," said Mrs. Day.

"Thanks again," said Ashlie.

She was starting to get annoyed. She was tired and just wanted to go to her apartment. Mrs. Day watched as Ashlie went up the stairs. Ashlie could hear her husband tell her to quit being nosy and shut the door. Ashlie chuckled. When Ashlie got to her apartment she set her bags down so she could unlock the door. Some times the lock stuck and she had to jimmy the key in it to open it. And this just happen to be just one of those times. She couldn't remember how many times she has told the manager about it. But it just seems like the words had just fallen on deaf ears. When she finally got the door open she walked in and turned around and pushed the door shut with her foot. She headed straight for the bedroom. She set her bags down on the floor and set the package on the bed. She was about to head to bathroom, when the phone rang. She sat down on the bed and picked up the phone.

"Hello," she said.

"Ashlie, when did you get home," said Skyler.

"I just walked in the door," she said. "And I was about to go in and take a pee when you called."

"Well you don't have to get so sarcastic," he said.

"I'm sorry Skyler, your right," she said. "I didn't have a very good trip home, but that's no excuse to snap your head off."

"Apology accepted," he said.

"So has anything new developed on the case since we last spoke?" she asked.

She started opening the package while Skyler explained a couple of new thing they found out. She tugged at the taped. Who ever had wrapped it made sure they had plenty of tape. She finally ripped her way threw the tape and opened the top. There were news paper clippings on top. The headlines said, "Mother stabbed to death by daughter." The next clipping said, "Daughter declared insane." There was a picture of Ashlie with her sister. Ashlie didn't hear what Skyler was saying as she pulled out a t-shirt from the box. It was cover with blood stains. Ashlie recognized the shirt. She screamed and dropped the shirt back in the box.

"Ashlie what's the matter!" asked Skyler. "Ashlie answer me he said with panic in his voice."

Ashlie finally managed to get her whits about her.

"Nothing I'm fine, I just saw a big hairy spider run across the floor," she said. "I'll be there in about an hour."

Before Skyler could say another word she hung up the phone. She started to pick up the box and move it when the phone rang. I told him I'd be there in an hour she said to herself as she picked up the phone.

"I told you I'd be there in an hour," she said.

"Did you get my package?" the voice on the other end said in a cackley voice.

Ashlie froze. Then she said in a shaky voice.

"What do you want, why are you doing this?" she asked.

"So many questions and so little time," the voice said.

"What do you mean so little time?" she asked.

"Don't worry it won't be long and all your questions will be answered," said the voice.

Then there was silence on the other end. Ashlie just stood there and shook. She had seen a lot of things and had been in a lot of situations where her life had been in danger, but she had never felt as scared and helpless as she did now. She had to tell someone. She knew now that she couldn't handle this along. She sat down on the bed and stared at the box. She was sitting there staring at the box trying to figure out what to do when there was a knock at the door. She darn near jumped out of her skin. She was going to ignore it when she hears a voice say, "Ashlie are you okay?" It was Skyler. She was never so glad to hear his voice in her life. She ran to the door and swung it open and threw her arms around his neck.

"Gee, I didn't realize you missed me so much," he said.

She pulled back and he could see the fear in her face.

"We need to talk," she said.

"Okay, about the case?" he asked.

"No, something else," she said. "But you've got to promise not to tell anyone about what I'm going to tell you, promise me."

"Okay, I promise, he said.

"Cross your heart and hope to die and all that stuff," she said.

"I said I promise," he said

She took his hand and lead him into the bedroom and over to the box on the bed.

"What is this, your box of tricks?" he asked.

She shot him a dirty look. Just kidding he said smiling. She wasn't amused with his jokes. She sat him on the bed and handed him the clipping. He got a puzzled look on his face.

"So explain, what this has to do with the case," he said.

"It doesn't," said Ashlie.

"Then what?" he asked.

"It's about me," she said. My mother hated me because I wasn't a boy, and she would beat me every day and remind me of how I screwed up everyone's life. It was my fault my dad left. This went on until one day she beat me, one to many times and I snapped and stabbed her with a large kitchen knife and killed her, at least that's what my sister tells me.

"You mean you don't remember?" asked Skyler.

"I blacked out and don't remember," said Ashlie.

"How do you know you did it?" he asked.

"My sister said she came home and found me holding my mom with the knife in her chest," answered Ashlie. "Why would she lie?"

Skyler didn't say anything. Next she pulled the shirt out of the box.

"This is the shirt I was wearing that day," she said.

He just looked at her funny and finally said, "You kept it?"

"No! I didn't keep it," she said raising her voice. "Obviously some else did. It came in the mail this morning. I've also received threatening letters and phone calls too."

"So why didn't you ask for help sooner?" he asked.

"Because I thought I could handle it by myself, until now," she said.

"We're partners, I thought we were supposed to stick together," he said in a low voice.

"Your right, I'm sorry," she said.

She just wanted him to pull her into his strong arms and hold her. She needed him so bad right now. She scooted closer toward him, hoping he would sense how she was feeling about him right now. Skyler leaned over and put his arms around Ashlie and pulled her into him. She buried her head into his chest. He smelled so good. She was getting turned on. He started kissing her on the neck and she started kissing his chest. Ashlie pulled away.

"We probably should get going," said Ashlie

"I know, but you turn me on," he said.

She just smiled at him and got up. Then the phone rang.

"See I told you so," she said.

Ashlie crawled across the bed and picked up the phone, "Hello," she said.

"Good afternoon Ashlie," the cackly voice said.

Skyler could see the fear in Ashlie's face.

"What do you want?" Ashley screamed into the phone.

"Well aren't we a little edgy," said the voice. "I just called to see if you enjoyed the package I sent you."

"Why don't you just show your ugly face, instead of being a chicken and hiding behind the phone?" Ashley screamed into the phone.

By this time Skyler had his ear up to the phone listening.

"All in good time my dear," said the voice. (Laughing into the phone).

Then the phone when dead. Ashley slammed the receiver down. Skyler held her tight. She started crying and shaking uncontrollably. He just held her, he couldn't think of the right words to say. He was never very good with words in situations like this. Finally he said, "Why don't I take that stuff down to the lab and have them analyze it, maybe they can come up with something."

"I don't think they'll find anything," said Ashlie.

"You never know," he said.

"I guess it can't hurt," she said.

Skyler reached into the box and took out the shirt; he just kept looking at it. Finally she said, "what?"

"Didn't you say you plunged the knife into your mother's chest?" he asked.

"Yea, that's what my sister said," answered Ashlie. Why do you ask?

"Well it seems like there would be a certain pattern on the shirt, and there's not," he said.

Ashlie really never looked at the shirt before. She actually never wanted to. All these years Ashlie never questioned what happened. She trusted her sister and took her word for it.

"So do you remember anything about what happened?" he asked.

"No," said Ashlie. "I've tried to remember even parts of what happened but nothing comes to me. I just believed what my sister said."

"What about the evidence at the crime scene," asked Skyler?

"I really don't know," answered Ashlie. All I remember is my sister holding me and then the police taking me in for questioning. Then they sent me away for a while to spend time with a physiatrist. She said I just snapped from the abuse and they released me into my sister's custody. No more was ever said about it. In fact I thought I put it all behind me until I started getting those phone calls and letters. I just don't know who would drag this all up.

"Probably some one you pissed off during your career," said Skyler.

"Maybe," she said. "They sure went to a lot of work to get back at me."

Ashlie and Skyler started to head out the door when the phone rang again. Ashlie froze in her steps. Skyler nudged her. She did not want to answer the phone. Reluctantly she walked over and picked it up. She was expecting that voice again.

"Are you and Skyler planning on coming to work any time soon?" asked Captain James.

"Yes, sir we're on our way right now," said Ashlie.

"Good, cuz this is not going to solve itself," he said sarcastically.

"Okay, sir goodbye," she said and hung up the phone.

"Captain?" said Skyler.

"Yep, and he's chomping at the bit," she said.

They hurried up and headed out to the car. They were in such a hurry that they forgot the box with the blood stained shirt in it. When they got down to the station Skyler remembered the shirt.

"Damn," said Skyler.

"What?" Asked Ashlie.

"We forgot the shirt," he said.

"Don't worry, we'll get it later," she said.

"I guess your right," he said. "It's not like it's going anywhere."

They got out of the car and went into the police station. When Ashlie got to her desk there was a stack of folders on it. She walked behind her desk and sat down and took a deep breath, and then she grabbed the folder on top. She opened it up and the first thing she saw was a picture of a man. He was dead and his privates had been removed. She was lost in thought when Skyler touched her on the shoulder. She jumped.

"I didn't mean to scare you," Said Skyler. "Pretty nasty aren't they."

"Yea," said Ashlie. "Did they ever figure out if the poor basters were dead before they were chopped on?"

"They're still not sure yet," he said.

"They sure are dragging there feet on this," she said. "Can you imagine having this done while you were still alive?"

"No, I don't ever want to think about it," he said. "It makes me hurt just looking at the pictures."

"Well at least we know it's a serial killer," she said. "Did they come up with a profile on this person?"

"Still working on it," he said.

"So, I wander what they're waiting for, this person to come in and give them the information?" she said sarcastically.

"You never know," said Skyler.

As they were there sitting and going over the files the captain walked up.

"Don't you two have anything better to do, than sitting around chatting?" he said.

"We were going over these files," answered Skyler.

"How many times do you need to go over them?" asked the captain.

"You never know what we might have missed," said Ashlie with sarcasm in her voice.

"You guys are detectives! Now go and detect something," he said raising his voice.

He stomped off to his office and slammed the door.

"Man, what's his problem?" asked Ashlie. "You'd think someone cut off his balls."

"It's his wife, she leads him around by the balls," said Skyler.

"Well she must be pinching them awful hard," she said. They both laughed. Ashlie picked up the files and said to Skyler, "Let's go get something to eat." He thought that was a good idea. They headed out the door. They decided to get some take out Chinese and go back to Ashlie's and go over the files. Ashlie felt that there was something in those files that they missed. She wanted to get this case solved before there was another murder. They stopped and picked up their food and headed to Ashlie's. She couldn't wait to get there, she was starving. When they got to the door of Ashlie's apartment, she knew something wasn't right.

"What's wrong?" asked Skyler.

"Someone was in my apartment," she said.

She showed Skyler were the door had been jimmied. He told her to wait there as he slowly pushed the door open. He looked around but didn't find anything. Ashlie asked the neighbors if they had seen anyone, but they said no. She went back to her apartment. She looked around but couldn't find anything missing. They sat down and ate. When they were done, she cleaned up. She told Skyler that they could go to the bedroom and lay the files out over the bed and study them. He told her that the only thing he wanted to lay out on the bed is her. She smiled and walked over to him and kissed him. He kissed her back passionately. That turned her on. She grabbed him by the hand and led him to the bedroom. They hadn't noticed that the box was gone, and in its place was a note. Skyler was about to push Ashlie down on the bed when he spotted the note. He grabbed her and pulled her back. He moved her to the side and reached down and picked up the note. Ashlie was stunned. She started to say, what the heck are you doing, when she saw the note in his hand. It said, "If you want this back you have to find me." PS. watch for my next victim. Ashlie couldn't believe that her past and the murders were tied together.

Now she was determined more than ever to solve this case. The killer just made it personal. Skyler put his arms around Ashlie and pulled her close, but she pushed away.

"What's the matter?" he asked.

"Nothing," she said. "I just think we should work on the case."

"If that's what you want," he said.

"Well you read the note," she said. "The killer is going to strike again."

"Your right," he said. "So let's get to work."

He stomped off into the other room. Ashlie just shook her head and said to herself, now I know why I never got involved with a man before. They're just like babies when they don't get what they want. When Ashlie got to the living room Skyler had a folder in his hand looking at it. Ashlie sat down beside him and picked up a folder. Skyler ignored her. Fine if that's the way you want it Ashlie thought to herself. She picked up the rest of the folders and went over to the kitchen table and set them down. She opened up each on and looked at them, but she couldn't concentrate. Her mind was on Skyler. Finally he said, "I'll see you tomorrow."

"Sure, no problem," Ashlie said. (Trying to act like she didn't care.)

"Okay, goodbye," he said.

He walked over to the kitchen table and kissed Ashlie on the cheek, and then he left. Now Ashlie felt bad about hurting his feeling. She thought about going after him and telling him she was sorry. Then she got to thinking about it and figured he was the one that owed her an apology. He was the one that was insensitive about her feelings.

Ashlie went back to the files. Maybe they would take her mind off of Skyler, she said to herself. There has to be a connection she thought. She was studying the pictures of the victims when the phone rang. She hurried up and answered it, thinking it might Be Skyler calling to apologize.

"Hello," said Ashlie. "Skyler if you're calling to apologize, I accept it."

"Oh how nice," said the voice. Ashlie froze. "I see I have your attention."

"What do you want?" asked Ashlie.

"I like that, right to the point," said the voice.

"Why can't you leave me alone!" said Ashlie.

"Oh, I can't do that just yet," said the voice. "You're the only one that can save me."

"What do you mean?" asked Ashlie.

"Soon you will find out," said the voice. "I'll call you tomorrow and tell you were to find the next victim."

Before Ashlie could say anything else the phone went dead. Damn she said. This person was starting to get on her nerves. Maybe it was someone from her childhood, she said to herself. Or maybe someone she arrested in the past. She wanted to pick up the phone and call Skyler. But she wanted him to come back because he wanted to, not because he felt he had to. She laid all the photos out next to each other and studied them. Then she noticed that they all had gray hair and blue eyes. They were all around they're late fifties. Then a thought came into her head: that she didn't know where it came from. That if her dad was still around, he would be about that age. She hadn't thought about her dad in years. She started thinking about where he was and what he was doing.

She actually didn't know if he was still alive. She thought about going down to the library and looking in the genealogy. What if he was alive? What would she say to him if she found him? She decided that it was a dumb idea and bushed it off. Ashlie took a deep breath and pushed her red hair out of her face. She heard that she inherited her red hair and blue eyes from her dad. And she had his temper to. Her sister was the splitting image of there mother. She got her brown hair and hazel eyes and also her mood swings. One day she was up and the next day she was down. It drove everyone crazy. She wondered if she married Skyler what their children would be like. Would they have her red hair and blue eyes and firery temper or Skyler's jet black hair and dark brown eyes and his laid back attitude? Or would they have little of both. She was lost in thought when the phone rang. Ashlie froze. She decided to let the answering machine get it. When it was done telling them to leave a message after the beep, Skyler started to speak. He started to say, "Ashlie I just called to apologize." Before he could finish she ran over and picked up the receiver. She said, "Skyler, hi."

"Ashlie? When you didn't answer, I thought you didn't want to talk to me," he said.

"No, it's not that, I thought it was that voice again," she said.

"Did they call you again?" he asked.

"Yea," she answered in a low voice.

"Well why didn't you call me!" he yelled into the phone.

"Because I didn't want you running over here because you thought you had to, I wanted you to be here because you wanted to be," she yelled back.

"Well I'm coming over right now," he said.

"No, you don't have to, I'm fine," she said.

"No you're not fine. If you were, you wouldn't have been afraid to answer the phone," he said.

"Okay, if it makes you feel better," she said.

She was too tired to argue with him. She hung up the phone and looked at the pictures. There had to be something else that tied all these cases together she said to herself. What can it be? Maybe the pathologist will have something more tomorrow. Ashlie decided to lie down on the couch and wait for Skyler. She closed her eyes and she didn't realize she dozed off until a loud knock on the door woke her up. She jumped up and in a daze went to the door and opened it without asking who it was. Skyler was standing there with an angry look on his face.

"What?" asked Ashlie half asleep.

"I can't believe you opened the door with out asking who was there," he said.

"Who else would it be? You said you were coming over," she said.

"What if I had been the killer," he said.

"Well I think I'm safer than you are, I don't have any balls," she said sarcastically.

"Very funny," said Skyler.

"I thought so," answered Ashlie. "Come on I don't want to fight. I'm too tired."

"Okay, you win," he said. "We'll talk in the morning."

He wrapped his arms around her and pulled her close and kissed her passionately.

She whispered in his ear, "Let's go to bed."

"Sounds good to me," he said.

She led him into the bedroom. They undressed each other. They made love. Then Ashlie went right to sleep, she was exhausted. Skyler kissed her on the cheek and told her goodnight and snuggled up to her and went to sleep.

CHAPTER 2

WHEN ASHLIE WOKE up Skyler was sitting up in bed staring at her.

"Good morning," he said.

She smiled and asked, "What are you doing?"

"Watching you sleep," he said.

"Why, it can't be too exciting," she said.

"It just that you're so beautiful I couldn't help myself," he said.

Ashlie blushed. She could feel her cheeks burning. He leaned over and kissed her and she kissed him back.

"We have to get up," she said.

"Just five more minutes," he protested.

"No, we need to get going on this case so we can get the captain off our backs," she said.

"Oh alright," he said. Ashlie got up and went into the bathroom to take a shower. I hope he doesn't want to take a shower with me, she thought to herself. She decided to take a real quick shower, hoping she'd be done before Skyler got up. Just as Ashlie was stepping out of the shower and wrapping the towel around her, Skyler walked into the bathroom.

"Already done?" he said. "I was hoping we could take a shower together."

"Sorry, I guess you weren't quick enough," she said.

"Why don't you let me dry you off," he said walking toward her.

"I'll tell you what, why don't you start your shower and I'll go fix us some breakfast," she said.

She smiled at him and walked out the door.

"Whatever," he said with disappointment in his voice.

Ashlie wished she could just get dressed, grab a quick bite to eat and head out the door. She wasn't sure if she really wanted a relationship with Skyler or not. It was cramping her lifestyle. She was use to coming and going as she pleased and not answering to anyone. She'd have to think long and hard about it and decide if it's worth it. Just as Ashlie set breakfast on the table, Skyler came out of the bedroom. They sat down and ate in silence. When Ashlie was done she got up and cleared the table. Skyler got up and helped. As Ashlie was washing the dishes the phone rang. She just stood there. Skyler went over and picked it up and when he said hello they hung up.

"Who was it?" she asked.

"I don't know, they hung up," he said.

"Maybe it was a wrong number," she said.

"Or maybe it was your weird caller," he said.

"Maybe," she said. "I guess they didn't want to talk to you."

Ashlie continues to wash the dishes. Skyler went back to helping her and the phone rang again. This time Ashlie went over and picked it up.

"Hello," she said.

"I see you have company," the voice said.

Skyler could see the fear in Ashlie's face.

"I'm sorry but you must have the wrong number," said Ashlie.

She slammed down the receiver.

"Must be your caller?" said Skyler.

"Yea, if they think they can harass me and I'm going to take it lying down, they have another thing coming," she said raising her voice.

"Calm down," he said.

"How can I calm down," said Ashlie. "You don't know what it's like to have someone harass you every waking moment. I'm going to make it my personal mission to hunt this person down and get them. Even if it kills me."

"Man they really are pissing you off, aren't they?" he said.

"Damn right they are," she said.

Just as Ashlie finished cleaning up the phone rang again. Ashlie let it ring until the answering machine kicked on. "You listen here bitch, I know you're there. If you know what's good for you, pick up the phone," the voice said. Ashlie started to move toward the phone when Skyler stopped her. He shook his head no. Ashlie didn't fight him. After a minute the phone went dead.

"You have to let them believe you're in control," said Skyler.

"I know your right," said Ashlie. But . . .

"No, if you cave in, then they're in control," he said.

"I really got to them didn't I?" she asked.

"Yea you did, that's what we want," he said. "We have to get them eating out of your hand."

The phone rang again. This time Skyler picked it up. It was the captain. They found another body. He said this one was different from the others; it had a note pinned to it. He wanted to see Ashlie in his office right away. Skyler and Ashlie put on their coats and headed for the door when the phone rang again, this time Ashlie picked it up, thinking it was the captain again.

"You should have answered the phone," the voice said.

"You know something, I'm really getting tire of you," said Ashlie raising her voice.

She slammed down the phone and walked out the door. I'm not answering the phone again tonight! Skyler closed the door and locked it. They got in the car and headed for the station. When they got to the station Ashlie just sat there in the car and stared out the window in silence.

"Are you okay?" asked Skyler, laying his hand on her shoulder.

"Yea, I'll be fine," she said, smiling at him. "She took a deep breath and said, I think I know why the captain wants to see me."

"Why?" he asked.

"The note, pinned to the body," she said. I think it was for me. "They were going to call and tell me where to find the next body. So I would find the note before anyone else. That's probably why they called."

"Well I guess we'll find out pretty soon," he said.

They got out of the car and headed for the station. When they got in, Ashlie headed for the captains office. She knocked on the door.

"Come in!" the captain yelled.

"You wanted to see me?" said Ashlie.

"You bet I did!" he said, raising his voice. "You want to explain this?"

He laid the note down on the desk in front of Ashlie. It was in a plastic evidence bag. The letters had been cut out and pasted on a white sheet of paper. Ashlie noticed red splatters on it. She assumed it was the victim's blood. The note said, "DEAR ASHLIE I DID THIS ONE ESPECIALLY FOR YOU. PS. THIS ONE WAS AWAKE." Ashlie got a sick feeling down in the bottom of her stomach. The poor bastard must've really suffered, she thought to herself.

"I don't know sir," she said.

"I think you do know!" he said yelling. "So you had better start talking or you'll be on suspension, WITHOUT PAY!"

"Well sir, I don't know where to begin," she said.

"How about the beginning," he said, lowering his voice a little.

"Well I've been getting these calls, and until the last couple of days I didn't know that this person calling me and the killer were connected," she said.

"Do you know why this person started calling you?" he asked.

"It has something to do with my past," she said.

"Your past?" he said.

"Yea, when I was fifteen they say I killed my mother," she said.

"They say?" he said, with question in his face.

"Yea, I don't remember doing it," she said. "I just remember holding my mom and crying. Everything else is blank. The physiatrist's said the trauma caused me to have amnesia. Even under hypnosis they couldn't get me to remember. They say I have it stored away in my brain and someday I'll remember. But so far I haven't."

"So who found you?" he said.

"My sister," she said.

"Well I think the first thing we need to do is tap your phone, so we can try and get a trace on this caller," he said. "Tomorrow morning we'll send some people over to set that up."

"Sounds good to me," she said.

"Do you keep in contact with your sister?" he asked.

"No, not really, I haven't talked to her in about 10 years," she said. "We didn't part on good terms. Ashlie could see the question in his face. Well she tried to control every inch of my life. And I couldn't handle it."

"Do you know were she lives?" he asked.

"Yea, she only lives a couple of miles from me," she answered. "I'll write her address down for you."

"Maybe you could talk to her," said the captain.

"No, I don't think so," said Ashlie raising her voice.

"I'm sure she has forgiven you by now," he said.

"I doubt it," she said. "I think her last words to me as I was walking out the door were, "If you ever show your face here again, I'm going kick your ass. Now does that sound like the word of a loving sister?"

"Well I guess not," he said. "I'll send someone else to see her tomorrow."

"I appreciate that," she said.

As Ashlie got up to leave the captain told her to be careful and keep her door locked. She thanked him for his concern and left. Skyler offered to drive her home. She sat there in silence thinking about the note and all that had been happening. It was almost too overwhelming. When they got to Ashlie's apartment, Skyler turned off the car and they just sat there quietly staring out the window. Finally Skyler turned to Ashlie and said, "Do you want me to stay the night?" She turned to him and said, "Yes, that would be nice." He smiled and leaned over and kissed her. She passionately kissed him back. She couldn't wait to get Skyler in bed. Despite all that was going on, it hadn't hurt her lust for sex and Skyler was real good at it. She had no complaints about him in that department. He defiantly was a good lover. When they got into the apartment Ashlie closed the door and locked it. She turned to Skyler and got a big smile on her face. They head for the bedroom.

It wasn't long after Ashlie falls asleep that she starts dreaming. She is walking thru the woods. She has a night gown on. It is very dark and the ground is cold on her bare feet. The leaves make a crunching noise as she walks down a path. An owl screeches in the tree and she jumps. She don't know why she is there, she just knows that she must keep going. She hears a rustling noise in the bushes and she spins around and a dark figure jumps out of the bushes and lunges for her. She screams and takes off running, but it seems like she's running in slow motion. But she just keeps going. This shadow is gaining on her. She tries to run faster and she trips over something in the path. As she tries to get up something grabs her leg and she turns around and comes face to face with a man. She screams and tries to get up. He says to her, "Help me." She looks at his face and it's Skyler. Ashlie screams NO! And bolts up in bed. Skyler wakes. Ashlie is sweating and shaking.

"Are you okay?" he asks.

"I don't know," she answered. "That dream it was so real."

"What was it about?" he asked.

"I'm not sure," she said. "But I think it had something to do with the murders and the killer."

"It was only a dream," said Skyler. "You're probably just dreaming about that stuff, because you've been working on it so much."

"Yea, you're probably right," she said.

She lay back down and Skyler cuddled up to her and held her in his arms. But Ashlie couldn't go back to sleep. That dream really scared her. She glanced at the clock on the stand beside the bed; it said 12:00 am. It's going to be a long night Ashlie thought to herself. After about an hour Ashlie couldn't hold out any longer and closed her eyes. When she woke up the sun was shining thru the window. She turned over and Skyler was gone. She smiled and figured he was in the kitchen fixing breakfast for them. She got up and put her robe on and wondered into the kitchen, but he wasn't there. But she found a note from him. It said, "I let you sleep, cuz I know you had a ruff night. I'll catch you later. Love Skyler. Just as she finished reading the note, the phone rang. She about jumped over the kitchen counter. Ashlie didn't know whether to answer it or not. What if it's Skyler she thought to herself? She picked it up on third ring.

"Well good morning," the voice said.

"What do you want?" Ashlie said angrily.

"Well is that any way to greet a friend," they said.

"You got a lot of balls calling me your friend," she said.

"You should be nice to me," said the voice.

"Yea, right," said Ashlie sarcastically.

"You don't get it do you," they said raising their voice.

"You got that right," she said. "What kind of sick son of a bitch goes around cutting men's privates off and letting them bleed to death."

"Don't you see," said the voice. "They can't hurt any women anymore."

"What your daddy fucked you, so now you're getting your revenge on all the other men in the world," she said angrily.

"Now you're getting it," said the voice. "By the way, if I were you I'd keep a close watch on that sexy man of yours."

"You'd had better even think of laying a finger on him, or I'll personally hunt you down and kill you myself," she yelled.

"I can't wait," said the voice.

The phone went dead. Ashlie slammed the receiver down and buried her head into her hands. The door opened and Skyler walked in. She looked up at him and he could see that she was upset.

"What's going on," he asked.

"I got another call," she said.

"Shit," he said. "I was hoping they would get the tap hooked up before they called again."

Ashlie just sat there thinking about what the voice. She begins to think that they were dealing with a very angry woman.

"So what are you thinking?" asked Skyler

"What?" said Ashlie?

She was lost in thought when Skyler spoke to her.

"I was wondering what you were thinking?" he said.

"Oh, nothing really," she said.

"It sure didn't look like nothing, by the look on your face," he said.

"Well I was trying to analyze what the caller said," she said. "It just didn't make sense."

"Well what did they say?" he asked.

"It's what it didn't say that bothers me," she said.

"Well maybe I can help you figure it out if you tell me what they said," answered Skyler.

"Maybe your right," said Ashlie. "How about we go get some breakfast and I tell you all about it."

"We don't have to," he said. "I stopped and picked some donuts and turnovers."

He reached into a bag pulled out a box from the bakery. Ashlie went to the cupboard and got out two plates. She set the plates on the table and Skyler brought the box over and sat down. He pushed it towards Ashlie, motioning for her to pick first. She lifted the lid of the box and pulled out two donuts and a turnover. They were still warm.

"They were just taking them out of the oven when I got there," said Skyler.

"Talk about good timing," she said.

"So are you going to tell me what they said?" asked Skyler.

"I'll try," said Ashlie. "It's complicated."

"Well why don't you give it your best shot," he said.

"Okay, here goes," she said." I think that it is a woman. (Skyler got a confused look on his face) Let me explain. The voice said that they cut of the privates of the men so they wouldn't hurt any more women. Then I asked, "what did your father do fuck you?" and they said now your getting it."

"How do you know it isn't a man, and his dad fucked him when he was a boy?" asked Skyler.

"I guess it woman's intuition," said Ashlie.

"I don't know," said Skyler. "I think we should leave our options open."

"I guess," said Ashlie, biting into a donut.

After she takes her last bite, she picks up her plate and sets it on the counter by the sink. She decides to go get dressed. Skyler follows her into the bedroom. She turns around and comes face to face with him. He leans over and kisses her. She kisses him back passionately. He pushes her over to the bed. They start to make love when the phone rang. After three rings Ashlie picked it up.

"Your man is sure sexy with no clothes on," said the voice.

Ashlie grabbed a blanket and covered herself. By the look on her face Skyler could tell it was the voice again.

"What do you want?" Ashlie stammered.

"Did you think about what I said before?" the voice asked.

"Yea, and did you hear what I said," she said raising her voice.

"I'm looking forward to the challenge," said the voice.

The phone went silent. Ashlie slammed down the receiver.

"If they think they're going to get to me, then they've got another thing coming," she said.

"It looks like they have," said Skyler. Ashlie just glared at him and got up. "Well you don't have to get pissed off at me."

"I'm not!" snapped Ashlie. She went over to the closet and got some clothes out and started getting dressed.

"What ever," said Skyler.

He got up and put his pants on. He started walking toward the door, when he turned around and said, "I'm going down to the station, see you later."

"Yea, okay. See you later," Ashlie mumbled.

Ashlie wanted to go see her sister, but she didn't want Skyler tagging along. She had some personal things she wanted to discuss with her. She decided not to call, she wanted to surprise her.

CHAPTER 3

*I*T WAS NOON and Skyler hadn't heard from Ashlie since he left her at her place. He decided to call and see what was up but no one answered. So he decided to go over there to see if she was okay. Skyler knocks on Ashlie's door, but no one answers the door. He yells, "Ashlie answer the door. But there is just silence. He goes down to her neighbors and knocks on the door. Mrs. Day answers the door.

"Hi, my name is Skyler," he said.

"Oh, your Ashlie's friend," she said smiling.

"Yea, have you seen her today?" he asked.

"Oh, I think she left around 10:00 this morning," she said. "She seemed to be in a hurry."

"She didn't say where she was going, did she?" he asked.

"No, why do you ask?" she said.

"She never showed up for work," he said.

"I hope she's fine," she said.

"Well thanks anyway," he said.

He turned around and went back up to Ashlie's apartment. He picked the lock and went in. He looked around for a note or something. But he couldn't find anything. He sat down on the sofa and tried to think of where she could be. I hope she didn't go off and do something stupid the said to himself. He knew how bull headed she could be. As he was sitting there lost in thought the phone rang. He got up and answered it thinking it might be Ashlie.

"Hello Skyler," said the voice.

"How did you know I was here?" he said.

"I know everything," said the voice. Are you looking for Ashlie?

"Were is she?" he said raising his voice.

"Calm down," said the voice. "If you do what I say, nothing will happen to her."

"If you harm one hair on her head," he said.

"You'll what?" said the voice. "I suggest you sit down and shut up and listen to what I say."

"Let me talk to her, so I know she is alive," he said in a low voice.

"I guess I could do that," said the voice.

They put Ashlie on the phone.

"Skyler," she said.

"Ashlie are you okay?" he asked.

"Yea, I'm fine," she said.

He could hear the fear in her voice. She tried to give him a hint, but they took the phone from her before she could say anything.

"Are you listening," said the voice.

"Yea, I'm listening," said Skyler.

"The first rule is no calling the cops," said the voice.

"Why am I not surprised by that," said Skyler. He was starting to get annoyed.

"The next rule is be where I tell you to be at the time I tell you," said the voice.

"Is that it," said Skyler.

"No, that's not it," said the voice. "I'll call you back tonight at 10:00p.m. I expect you to answer on the second ring."

Before Skyler could say anymore the phone went dead. Skyler slammed down the receiver and got up and paced back and forth thinking of what to do next.

"Well it looks like I got his attention," said the voice to Ashlie.

"Why are you doing this?" asked Ashlie. You're my sister.

"You still don't get it do you?" she said.

"No, I must've have missed something, why don't you clue me in," said Ashlie Sarcastically.

"It's all about daddy," she said.

"What does he got to do with it?" asked Ashlie.

"He loved me more than you and momma," she said. "Momma was jealous of that love, so she sent him away. She knew that when you got old enough that he would come to your room like he did mine and love you more too."

"You mean daddy had sex with you?" asked Ashlie.

"It had nothing to do with sex," she said raising her voice. "We made love."

"Love?" said Ashlie. "That's not love, its incest."

"You shut up," said her sister.

She slapped Ashlie across the face. Ashlie felt her face sting as her hand stuck her face. Ashlie didn't know how sick her sister really was.

"What are you going to do to Skyler," asked Ashlie.

"He's a man, I won't treat any different that the others," she said.

"Why are you doing this, Dee?" asked Ashlie. "Can't you leave Skyler out of this? This is between you and me."

"You took something from me, now I'm going to take some thing from you," said Dee. Momma paid the price, when she took Daddy from me. (Ashlie got a puzzled look on her face) That's right little sister, I killed momma not you. I drugged you, and then I killed the bitch. It was so easy. Now I'm going to win Skyler's confidence, and then I'll seduce him and then kill him. Ashlie's head started spinning; it was all too much for her to take in. The room went black. That's right little sister, you go to sleep. And when you wake up it will all be over. Now I've got to get ready for my rendezvous with your boyfriend. She left the room. Dee made sure the door was locked and secure. She didn't want Ashlie messing up her plans.

Skyler decided to head down to the station to see if the lab work came back on the victims. As he walked into the station the captain was waiting for him. He wanted to see him in his office.

"Yea what's up," said Skyler closing the door behind him.

"Where's you partner?" asked the captain.

"Well I'm not sure, but I'm working on it," answered Skyler.

"What do you mean, your not sure," said the captain raising his voice.

"She's been kidnapped," said Skyler in a low voice.

"Kidnapped!" yelled the captain.

"Could you kept your voice down," said Skyler. "They threatened to kill her if I went to the police. They're suppose to call tonight and tell me were to meet them."

"We'll get that tap on the phone, so we can trace it," said the captain.

"You'd better let me do that, so they don't get suspicious," said Skyler.

"That's fine, just make sure you keep them on the phone long enough to get a trace," he said.

Skyler decided to head straight back to Ashlie's place to set up the tap. He wanted to make sure everything was working okay before the call. When he got to her apartment he turned off the car and sat there for a few minutes and stared out the window. He was worried about Ashlie. He didn't know what he would do if something happened to her. He loved her so much. He got out of the car and head up the stairs to Ashlie's apartment. On the way up Mrs. Day stuck her head the door and asked if he had found Ashlie. He answered her with a quick no and continued up the stairs. She went back into her apartment mumbling. Skyler didn't mean to be so short with her. He said to himself, "I'll make up to her later when this is all over. When Skyler got to the apartment the answering machine was flashing, there was one message on it. Skyler pushed the button to play it back. Skyler couldn't believe his ears, it was Ashlie's sister. She wanted to come and see Ashlie and talk over some things. She would stop by around 7:00 pm tonight. She hoped she didn't mind. I thought they weren't talking Skyler said to himself. OH, well I guess I'll talk to her.

When Ashlie awoke she was alone. She was surprised that she wasn't tied up or something. She looked around the room. It was small and damp. The floor was dirt. I must be in a basement Ashlie said to herself. There were no windows. The only way in or out was the door. She got up slowly. Her head was still a little woozy. She slowly walked over to the door and tried the handle, it wouldn't turn. It was worth a try she said to herself. She pushed on the walls to see how solid they were. They didn't budge. She went back over and sat on the bed. If had something, I could knock a hole in the wall she thought to herself. They were only sheetrock. She knew she had to keep a clear head if she was to get out of here and save Skyler. She knew that Dee could never seduce Skyler, he loved Ashlie to much. And that would only piss Dee off more.

Skyler lay down on the sofa and closed his eyes. It wasn't long and he had dozed off to sleep. He started to dream about Ashlie. She was walking toward him. Her hair was flowing down over her shoulders. She looked like an angel. She has a smile on her face. She reached out for him, she kept walking towards him. As she got closer he could see blood stains on her chest. Tears were running down her face. As she got closer he could see the butcher knife in her hand. She raised it up and plunged it into his chest. He yells NO! And woke up sweating and trying to catch his breath. As Skyler is sitting there trying to gather his thoughts the phone rang. He almost jumps out of his skin. Dam phone he says to himself. He goes over and picks it up.

"Hello," says the woman. Is Ashlie there?

"No, she isn't," says Skyler. "My I take a message."

"This is Ashlie's sister, Dee, I left a message earlier," she said.

"Well she hasn't come home yet," said Skyler. "I'll have her call you when she gets in."

"Maybe I could come over and wait for her," she said. "It's kind of important."

"I don't know when she'll be home," said Skyler.

"That's okay, I'll be there in a little bit," she said.

Before Skyler could say anymore the phone went dead. Sure is pushy bitch Skyler said to himself. I can see why Ashlie had to get away from her. Skyler decided to fix him something to eat while he waited for her to show up. He managed to scrounge up enough food to make a sandwich.

He got a beer out of the frig and took it and the sandwich over to the sofa and sat down. He knew that Ashlie would be pissed at him for eating in the livingroom on the sofa. I guess what she didn't know wouldn't hurt her he said. He picked up the remote and turned on the TV. He flipped thru the channels trying to find something good to watch. Most of the movies were reruns. He flipped off the TV and looked at the clock. It read 6:30 pm. Just as he finished his last bite of sandwich there was a knock at the door. He picked up his plate, brushed the crumbs off the sofa and went into the kitchen. He set the plate on the counter next to the sink and went to answer the door. He opened the door and there was Dee standing there with a smile on her face.

"Hi, I'm Dee, Ashlie's sister," she said.

"Hi, I'm Ashlie's boyfriend," Said Skyler.

Before he could invite her in, she pushed her way past him and took off her coat and made herself at home.

"Ashlie never mentioned how handsome you were," she said.

"I didn't know she talked to you," Skyler said with question in his voice.

"Oh, she called me the other day," said Dee. "I was surprised. We hadn't talked in years. Then all of sudden out of the blue I get a call. Who a thought."

"Yea, who a thought," said Skyler. "But like I said earlier, she's not here."

"That's okay," she said. "Maybe you could tell me about you."

Skyler felt uncomfortable with Dee there. The clothes she was wearing didn't cover much.

"You know," said Dee, "Ashlie had better keep a close eye on you; I just might snatch you away."

"I don't think she has to worry about that," said Skyler in a low voice.

Dee heard what he said and that infuriated her. She always thought she was prettier and could get any man she wanted. She walked over and leaned up against Skyler; she grabbed his hand and shoved it down her shirt. As he jerked his hand out, her shirt came unbuttoned and her breasts were exposed. She just laughed and took her shirt off.

"I think you had better leave," he said.

"Don't knock it until you tried it," she said.

She unzipped her skirt and dropped it to the floor, she was wearing no panties. She walked toward the sofa where she had laid her purse. She reached in and pulled out a revolver and pointed it at him. Drop you pants she said. Skyler didn't know what to think.

"You gotta be kidding?" he said.

"I'm dead serious," she said.

He unzipped his pants and dropped them to the floor. The boxers to, she said. They hit the floor. She smiled and said, "nice equipment." She told him to go into the bedroom. She made him lay on the bed. She crawled on top of him. She pointed the gun in his face and said, "I want it hard or I'm going to blow your head off. Skyler had to think fast. There was no way he was going screw that ugly bitch. She rubbed back and forth on him trying to get him hard. She started getting mad. I said get it hard, she yelled. Skyler reach up and grabbed the gun. She pulled the trigger and it went off just missing his head. He punched her in the face and knocked her off of him. The gun went flying across the floor. Skyler got up and ran over and picked it up. She lay on the bed and didn't move. Must've knocked her out he said. He went into the other room and got his pants. He pulled them on and went back into the bedroom to put the handcuffs on Dee and she was gone. "Son of a Bitch," said Skyler. The bedroom window was open and the curtains were blowing from the breeze. Skyler went to the window and looked out to see if he could see her. But she was long gone. He still had an hour before the kidnapper was suppose to call.

CHAPTER 4

*D*EE KNEW SHE had to move Ashlie somewhere else. She blew it and knew the cops would be swarming her house. She had to think of a good place to hide her. Ashlie was sitting on the bed when she heard footsteps above. Dee must be home she thought to herself. Then she heard someone come down the stairs. The handle turned on the door, the door opened. Dee stood in the door with a smile on her face.

"You'll never guess who I was with," she said.

"You know Dee, I'm not really in mood for you little guessing games," said Ashlie annoyed.

"Okay I'll tell you," she said. Skyler, "He's got one hot bod. He said to tell you hi."

"Yea, right," said Ashlie.

"You don't believe me," she said. "Then were did I get these."

She dangled his boxer shorts in front of Ashlie's face. Ashlie's face turned red with anger. She started to get up. Dee pushed her back down. Now you believe me, don't you?

"You could have got those anywhere," said Ashlie.

"Your right I could've, but I didn't," she said. "He was very cooperative. I think he enjoyed it as much as I did."

"I think you're a lying bitch!" said Ashlie.

Dee just stood there and laughed. Ashlie wanted to rip her throat out.

"I'll be back in a minute," said Dee. "I've got a phone call to make."

When Dee came back she told Ashlie they were leaving. Ashlie figured she would wait for the right moment and escape. As Dee was putting Ashlie in the car Ashlie slammed the door on her hand. Dee screamed. Dee managed to get her hand out of the door and Ashlie slammed it shut and locked it. Then she reached around and locked all the doors. She started to scoot over to the drivers set when she noticed there were no keys. Dee leaned over and looked in the driver's window and dangled the keys and smiled. She started to unlock the driver's door, just as she started to get in Ashlie unlocked her door and opened it and jumped. She took off running. She didn't even look behind to see if Dee was behind her. She could hear her cussing and screaming. Ashlie ducked behind some bushes, she needed to catch her breath. As she sat there trying to catch her breath, she tried to take in all that happened. Her head started spinning. I have to stay calm she said to herself. She hadn't realized how sick her sister was. She needed to get to a phone and try to get a hold of Skyler, before Dee tried to hurt him. Ashlie slowly got up and peeked up over the bushes to see if Dee was coming. Just as her head popped up over the bush a car was slowly coming down the street. Ashlie quickly got down, but it was too late. Dee spotted her. She jerked the steering wheel to the right; it jumped the curve and went across the lawn toward the bush. Ashlie jump out of the way just before the car ran over the bush. Ashlie could see the look on Dee's face. Dee slammed the car into reverse and backed up. Ashlie got up and ran between two houses and into an alley. She wasn't sure which way to go, until she saw the headlights from Dee's car. Ashlie climbed a fence and jumped into the back of a yard.

I hope they don't have a mean dog she said to herself. If I can get a look at the house numbers and street Address I could figure out were I was, Ashlie thought to herself.

Skyler was on his own adventure. He called up the station and told them to meet him at Dee's house. They wanted to know what was going on. He said he would explain when they got there. He didn't want to broadcast over the whole station that he got caught with his pants down. He figured that they would find out sooner or later. He wanted it to be later. When they got to the house he told the other detectives that Dee had pulled a gun on him and tried to shoot him. They knocked on the door but no one answered. They kicked it in. They had their weapons drawn. They looked around but she wasn't there. One of the police officers found the door to the basement. Skyler told two officers to stay up stairs and keep watch while he and the detectives went down. It was dark so they used their flashlights. When they got to the bottom there was a light hanging from the ceiling with a chain. Skyler checked it to see if it worked. He pulled the chain and it came on. When he let go it swung back and forth casting shadows around the room. He spotted a door. He walked over to it and slowly opened it. It was the room that Dee had kept Ashlie in. Skyler was looking around when one of the detectives yelled for him to come see something. He took one last look around the room and left. He went to see what was so important. He couldn't believe his eyes when he walked into the room. In the middle of the room was a table, like they used in the operating room or morgue. There was a sink. And by the sink was disinfectant and scrubs. On a tray was scalpels and alcohol. Over on the far wall was jars, like you'd use in canning, but what was in the jars almost took his breath away. It was the penis and testicles of the men that had been murdered. The jars had been labeled. Each one had the man's name and when he died on it. The one that really caught his eye was the one labeled Daddy. No it couldn't be, Skyler thought to himself. She couldn't be that sick. They decided not to touch anything until they got a search warrant. They knew they had they're killer. Then it hit Skyler, if Dee was the killer, then she was the one who kidnapped Ashlie. Why would she do this to her own sister? Skyler told the other detectives to go get the warrant he had something he had to do. He didn't know that Ashlie had escaped. He headed to the park were Dee had told him to go.

As Dee was driving around she realized that she had told Skyler were to meet her. She figured he didn't know that she didn't have Ashlie. She would go meet him and kill him and then go find Ashlie and get rid of her too. Then she started thinking that if she let Ashlie live that Ashlie would suffer more, because Skyler would be dead. She liked that idea better. Dee stopped the car and turned around. Where is she going Ashlie said to herself? Then it dawned on her, Dee was going after Skyler. Ashlie was more determined than ever to save him. Ashlie started running at a steady pace. Once she figured out where she was she knew she wasn't to far from her Apartment. Twenty minutes later she was at the bottom of the steps leading up to her apartment. She stood there for a minute to catch her breath. Just as she was about to go up the steps Mrs. Day stuck her head out the door. Please not now Ashlie thought to herself. She could hear Mr. Day yelling at her to mind her own business.

"Hello, Mrs. Day," said Ashlie.

"That nice you man you was with, was asking questions about you," she said.

"Do you know where he is?" asked Ashlie.

"No, he left here in a hurry a little while ago," she said.

"Did he say where he was going?" asked Ashlie.

"He was in such a hurry I didn't get to ask," she answered.

"Okay, Thanks a lot, you have a good night," said Ashlie.

She ran up the stairs to her apartment. She grabbed the spare key she kept above the door and unlocked it. She turned on the light and looked to see if Skyler might have written it down. But she couldn't find anything. She picked up the phone and called the station. She asked if they knew where he was. Nobody seemed to know. She was about to hang up when someone yelled into the phone.

"Ashlie, is that you? Where have you been!" it was the captain. Shit! She said to herself.

"Yea, captain, it's a long story," she said.

"Well I'm all ears!" he yelled.

"I can't explain right now, Skyler's life could be in danger," she said. "I need to know where he is."

"No, want you need to do is get your butt in here right now!" he yelled.

"I'm sorry captain, no can do," she said.

Before he could say another word she hung up. As she hung up the phone she noticed a piece of paper missing from her tablet by the phone. It was a brand new tablet she hadn't used it yet. She grabbed the pencil next to it and started to rub over the word pressed into the paper. It said, "go to the parking lot, get out of the car, and walk up the trail until you come to a clump of trees and a big boulder." Ashlie thought for a minute and then said out loud I know where that is. She would have to go there on foot. Her car was at Dee's. At least it wasn't too far away. Besides that way she could sneak up on her.

When Dee got to the park Skyler was already there waiting for her. He figured he would hide in the trees and wait until she came walking up the path and surprise her. But she decided to take a different way and double back on him and surprise him.

Ashlie was running down the street when she spotted a police cruiser. She darted behind a tree until it passed. She figured the captain had sent it to her apartment to pick her up and bring her in for an ass chewing. Not this time captain she said to herself. After the cruiser was out of sight she took off running again. It was hard to see. It was pitch black. There was no moon out. The only thing guiding her was the street lights. She finally spotted the park. When she got to the parking lot she saw Dee's car and Skyler's car. She looked in both cars for a flashlight. She found a small one in Skyler's car. As she was getting out she noticed that the car was leaning to one side. She shined the light on the left front tire, it was flat. After a close inspection she noticed the slash in the tire. Dee must've done it, she said to herself. She thought about changing it, but she was more worried about Skyler. She turned off the flash light and hurried up the path. She started up the path and tripped over something. Oh God, she thought to herself, I hope it's not human. She shined her light; it was just a large stick. She picked it up, it could come in handy. She got up headed towards the trees. As she got closer she quietly stepped towards the trees. She couldn't see anything. I hope I'm not to late she thought. Just as she walked past a big pine tree someone grabbed her and threw her to the ground. She let out a scream and started swinging the stick. On the second swing it connected with someone. They let out a howl.

"Skyler, is that you?" she said.

"Yea," he moaned.

"Oh my god, I'm so sorry," she said.

"And I was worried about your sister," he moaned.

"That's not funny, I came up here to save you," she said annoyed.

"How by knocking me out, so it would be easier for her to neuter me," he said sarcastically.

"I said I was sorry," she said.

As they were arguing they hear someone coming. They knew it had to be her. They moved over by the boulder and crouched down. Skyler was still moaning. Ashlie motioned for him to be quiet. Pretty soon Dee came out behind the trees onto the trail.

"If you want to see Ashlie again, you had better come out," she said.

Skyler motioned for Ashlie to double back and sneak up on her, while he got her attention. He stood up and walked towards her.

"Where is she?" he asked.

"Show me your hands," she said. "He held up his hands."

"Okay I did what I was told, now where is she?" he asked again.

"She's in a safe place, if you go with me I'll take you to her," she said.

Ashlie double backed and went behind the trees, she snuck up behind Dee and raised her stick to hit her. It was as if she had eyes in the back of her head. She turned around and grabbed the stick as it came down towards her head. They struggled and went down on the ground. Dee managed to push the stick across Ashlie's throat. Ashlie was in the wrong position to push up on the stick. Dee pushed harder, Ashlie gasped for air. Skyler ran over and grabbed Dee and pulled her off of Ashlie. Ashlie rolled over and coughed and gasped. Dee lunged at Skyler; He hit her and sent her rolling down an embankment. He went after her, but when he got down there she was gone. He went back up to make sure Ashlie was okay. When she finally got her breath she asked where Dee was. I don't know he said. She disappeared. He helped Ashlie up and they went down the embankment to look for Dee, but she had vanished into the night. They headed back to the car. They would look for her later. They knew as long as she was out there no one was safe.

Dee crouched down and hid in the bushes until Ashlie and Skyler left. Then she got up and brushed herself off. They won't get away with this, she said to herself. They will pay dearly. She headed back to her car. She waited until they left in Skyler's car and then she went and got in her car. She reached into her pocket to get her keys, but they weren't there. They must've fallen out when I rolled down the embankment she said to herself. She got out of her car and went back up the trail to find her keys. As she walked she started thinking of ways to bait Skyler into coming after her, so she could kill him. Ashlie would suffer then.

As Skyler drove, Ashlie just sat quietly and stared out the window. She was in shock. She didn't know what to say. She didn't know where to begin. So she just sat there quietly and thankful that Skyler was okay. She wished they could go back to her place and crawl into bed and hold each other. But she knew until her sister was caught that there would be no peace in they're lives. When they got to the station Skyler tuned off the car and turned to Ashlie. He held out his arms and she embraced him and buried her head into his chest.

"Do you know if your father is still alive?" he whispered into her ear.

"I don't know," she said. "Why do you ask?"

"Well you sister is sicker that we thought," he said. She pulled back and gave him a puzzled look. "We found in her basement a room with an operating table and some jars with parts of the men that were murdered. The jars were labeled with their name and date they were murdered. (He took a deep breath and continued) One of the jars was labeled "Daddy".

"But none of the men recovered was my dad," she said.

"How do you know?" asked Skyler.

"Because I've seen pictures of him," she said. "The men were about the same age as my dad would have been, but that's it."

"You don't suppose she has him in her house still?" said Skyler.

"I wouldn't even venture a guess about that right now," said Ashlie. They got out of the car and headed into the station. The captain was waiting for them. He wanted to see them both in his office. Ashlie couldn't tell if he was angry or just wanted to talk and right now she really didn't care. She was too tired to care one way or the other. When they got to his office Ashlie collapsed into a chair. The captain sat down behind his desk, but he didn't stay there very long. He didn't say two words and he was up pacing the floor. He needs to cut back on the caffeine Ashlie thought to herself.

"So what are you guys going to do to catch this killer?" he asked.

"Well were working on a plan sir," said Skyler.

Ashlie shot him a funny look.

"Well what is it?" he asked.

"Well were going to need bait," answered Skyler.

"What Kind of bait?" he asked.

"Well, it seems she has a fond attraction to me," said Skyler.

"I don't think so," said Ashlie raising her voice.

"It's the only way we're going to catch her," said Skyler.

"Sounds good to me," said the Captain. "Just make sure you wear a wire so we can come in if you need help. By the way here is your search warrant."

"Thanks, but I think well wait until we catch her," said Skyler. Ashlie and the Captain looked at him funny. "Well I think that's were we'll probably arrest her, so we don't want to scare her off."

"I don't think she'll be dumb enough to go back there," said Ashlie.

"But I think she will," said Skyler.

"Why would she do that?" asked Ashlie.

"She has an attachment to the place," he said. "After we arrest her I think well find out why."

Skyler called the police cruiser watching Dee's house to pull back. They thought that was weird but did what they were told. Skyler and Ashlie left the station. Skyler thought it would be a good idea to go back to his place. He figured Dee might call him there. At least he was hoping she would. He figured she wouldn't waste any time. On the way there Ashlie asked him how Dee ended up with his boxer shorts. His face turned bright red. He didn't really want to talk about it. But he knew sooner or later he would have to. So he figured no time like the present. He told Ashlie that Dee showed up at her apartment and held a gun on him and tried to rape him, but he managed to get the gun from her and she escaped out the window. He assured her nothing happened. Ashlie believed him. She felt sorry for him. She knew it must've been embarrassing for him. But she still couldn't stifle her laugh. Skyler glared at her. I'm sorry she told him. But I'm trying to picture you standing there with your pants around your ankles. She promised she wouldn't ever mention it again. He told her that he didn't see any humor in it. She apologized. But he wondered how sincere she was.

CHAPTER 5

WHEN DEE GOT to the spot were she went over the embankment she got down on her hands and knees and felt around for her keys. It was to dark to see anything, so she knew the only way to find them was by feel. As she was feeling around a light shined in her eyes. It startled her.

"Are you okay, Miss?"

Dee looked up to see a man with a flashlight on top of the embankment.

"I lost my car keys," she said.

"Would you like some help?" He asked.

Perfect she thought to herself, another victim.

"Yea that would be great," she said.

As he climbed down the embankment Dee noticed the badge on his coat. He was a park ranger. She got nervous and started digging around for her keys. As she was fumbling around in the dirt and leaves she felt something, it was her keys. Thank god she thought to herself. She got up and dangled her keys.

"I found them," she said.

"Great," he said.

"Well thanks for your help," she said.

She started up the hill.

"Would you like me to walk you to your car?" he asked.

She started to say no, but changed her mind.

"Sure, that would be nice," she said.

She waited up on the trail for him. When he got up there, they started down the trail.

"My name is Dan," He said.

Dee didn't say anything.

Then he said, "Do you have a name?"

Dee didn't want to give him her real name, so she told him her name was Ann. He kept asking her questions and it was starting to piss her off. When they got to her car she asked him if he was married. He said yes. So she asked him why he was hitting on her. He said that his wife only liked to have sex once a month so he just went else where to get it. Dee said to herself he'll make a good candidate. He was just like all the others, adulters. She asked him over to her place for a drink. He agreed to follow her home. Dee decided to play with this one first, then whack him. She got in her car and started it up. She put into drive and turned around and headed back towards the main road. She made sure she obeyed the law; she didn't want to draw any unwanted attention. When she got to her place she drove real slow to make sure there was no police there. It was all clear so she pulled into the drive way, She got out and opened the garage door. She got back in her car and pulled into the garage. She motioned for Dan to pull his truck in side. He thought that was a strange request. But he didn't argue. He was there after one thing only. When he pulled in she closed the door. He turned off his truck. She walked over to it and opened the door, he got out. She turned around and he grabbed her by the arm and pulled her close. He started groping her. She told him not here. He let go of her.

When they got the kitchen she told him to have a seat and she would get the drinks. He looked around and notice that she wasn't the best housekeeper, he wasn't there to inspect her house keeping skills anyway, he thought. He asked to use the bathroom. On his way he decided to look for her bedroom. When he got to Dee's bedroom he stood there looking at the queen size bed thinking about the fun he was going to have in it. As he was lost in thought Dee came up behind him and taps him on the shoulder. He darned neared jumped out of his skin.

"How about we go sit on the bed and get comfortable," she said.

"Sounds like a plan to me," he said smiling.

"Good, now you get real comfortable," she said. When he sat down on the bed she handed him his drink. She sat hers down on the side table. As he sat there drinking his drink she started undoing his pants. When she got his pants off he started feeling dizzy.

"I don't feel so good," he said.

"Date rape drug," she said smiling.

"What, what are going to do to me?" he said slurring his words.

"You won't feel a thing till you wake up," she said. "That'll teach you to cheat one your wife. This is for her. You're a creep just like the others."

When he was passed out she went and got a wheel chair out of the closet and rolled it over to the bed. She really had to struggle with this one, he was bigger that the others. But she managed to get him in it. She wheeled him to the basement door. She opened it and turned the wheel chair backwards and eased it down the stairs. When she got to the bottom she left him there and went up stairs and locked the door. She went back down and wheeled him into her special room. She dropped the operating table down low and laid him on it. She stripped him naked and strapped him down. He still had a hard on. Shame I have to cut this one off it's a nice size. I guess I'll have to get little bigger jar she said to herself.

She walked over to a closet and opened it. So what do you think Daddy? I think he's got a bigger one than you, she said. So do you want to watch? She walked into the closet and wheeled out a corpse and set it next to the right side of Dan's head. Then she went over to the sink and started scrubbing. She put on a white jacket and some surgical gloves. She walked back over to the table and picked up a scalpel. She put her mask on, and then she remembered her jar, so she went to closet and retrieved it. Then she asked, "Do think this one will do, daddy?" Okay thanks, I think your right. She pressed the scalpel against Dan's testicals and made an incision blood run everywhere. Must've got a vein she said to herself, she kept cutting until they were laying in her hand, she dropped them in the jar. As she started cut on his penis, he started to wake up.

"Oh, I see you coming around," she said. "I'm almost thru, it shouldn't hurt much."

He tried kicking his feet, but she had them strapped down.

"What the hell are you doing!" he screamed.

"Now if you don't stop yelling I'm gonna have to tape your mouth shut," she said in a low voice. "Besides daddy doesn't like it when you yell. Dan turned his head to the right to see a dead man staring him in the face. He let out a loud scream."

Dee went over and got some duct tape and ripped a peace off and put it over his mouth. See I told you so she said. She went back and picked up the scalpel and continued to cut. The tape muffled his screams of pain. When she was all done she dropped it in the jar and put the lid on it. She labeled it and held it up in front of Dan and smiled. Then she turned to the corpse and said, "See I conquered another one, what do you think of that?" She went over and put it on the shelf with the others. Then she went over to the corpse and hugged it and gave it a big kiss on the lips. When she turned around to look at Dan he was dead. "Poor baby," she said. She leaned over and kissed him. I guess your sex days are over with aren't they? Well daddy it's time for you to go back to your room. Dee wheeled him back to the closet and closed the door. She when over to the table and started cleaning up the blood. My, my you're a bleeder she said to Dan. She got the blood cleaned up. And then she took the straps off of him. She lowered the table and put him the wheel chair. She knew exactly what she was going to do with him.

Ashlie and Skyler were waiting at his place for Dee to call. Skyler decided to fix them a snack to eat when the phone rang. It startled them. Skyler went over and picked it up.

"Hello," he said.

"Skyler, this is the captain, we need you down here at the station," he said.

"What's up?" asked Skyler.

Ashlie could tell it wasn't Dee.

"When you guys get down here I'll explain it to you," he said.

When he hung up the receiver he looked at Ashlie.

"What's up?" asked Ashlie.

"I don't know," said Skyler. "It was the captain and he wants us down at the station. It sounded really important."

Skyler started putting things away, when Ashlie jumped up and grabbed the bag of chips. She reached in and grabbed a handful. Skyler just looked at her and she said she was hungry. After he cleaned up they headed out the door. It didn't take them long and they were at the station. The captain was waiting for them in his office.

"What's going on captain?" asked Skyler.

"A woman called in, her husband never came home from work," said the captain.

"Maybe he went out with some friends for a drink," suggested Ashlie.

"Not according to his wife," said the captain. "She said he don't drink on his work days."

"So where does he work?" asked Skyler.

"He's a park ranger," said the captain. "He patrols the park that you were in tonight. Here's the search warrant on your sisters house. Were not going to wait for her to contact you. We're gonna go ahead and pick her up. I hope were not too late."

Ashlie got a grim look on her face. She had a strong feeling that they were way to late. Skyler picked up the search warrant. He and Ashlie walked out of the captain's office. The captain stuck his head out door and told them to take back up with them. Ashlie hoped that there wouldn't be any trouble. She hoped that Dee would surrender peacefully. But knowing her sister it probably wouldn't happen. Skyler and Ashlie took two police cruisers with them. When they got to Dee's house it was quiet and dark. But they weren't taking any chances. They approached it cautiously. They were just about to check the front door, when they heard a loud noise. They turned around to see a pickup truck crash thru Dee's garage door. They couldn't tell who was driving it. But could tell there were two people in it. As it sped down the street Dee screamed out the window, "catch us if you can." Ashlie could hear the echoes of her laughter as she disappeared out of site. It sent chills up the back of her neck. Skyler motioned for one of the cruisers to go after her and to make sure they called for back up.

Skyler and Ashlie entered the house. They were being careful. They weren't sure if Dee had traps set or not. They headed for the basement door. Skyler knew that if anything happened it would be there. They eased there way down the stairs. When they got to the bottom Skyler remembered the light hanging from the ceiling, he pulled the chain and turned it on. He headed straight for the room that they had found earlier. When they walked in the smell almost took Ashlie's breath away.

"What is that smell?" asked Ashlie.

"Death," answered Skyler.

Ashlie didn't particularly care for that answer. She walked over to the shelf where Dee kept her specimens. She picked up one and was studying it when Skyler tapped her on the shoulder. She almost dropped it on the floor. She turned around and gave him a dirty look. Sorry he said. As she stood there studying it. It finally dawned on her what she was looking at. She set it down. She felt her stomach getting queasy. Skyler walked over to the closet where Dee kept her jars and he swung open the door. The smell darn near knocked him off his feet. As he got a closer look he saw where the smell was coming from. It the corner propped up was a corpse. Ashlie went over to see what he was looking at. Before she got there he grabbed her and led her away. That made her more curious. She really wanted to see what was in there now. But Skyler wouldn't let her near the closet. He told that they shouldn't touch anymore stuff until they get a forensic team in here to get evidence. The smell was starting to get to her anyway. She told him that she was going outside. He decided he'd better go up to. As they were heading towards the front door Ashlie noticed a photo Album on a stand in the hall way. It said, Family Album on the front of it. Ashlie picked it up and pressed it against her chest and walked towards the door. She recognized the album from when she was younger. She loved looking at the pictures. Ashlie and Dee would sit and talk and look at all the pictures. Sometimes she missed those days when things were okay. When the only thing she had to worry about was getting to school on time and doing her home work. She didn't know why, but she felt she needed to save her sister. Maybe because she was the only family she had left. And even though Dee had done what she had done she was still her sister. Ashlie went over to her car and laid the album in the front seat. She knew what she had to do. She had to find her sister; she was the only one that could help her.

Skyler was busy discussing things with the officers, so Ashlie slipped by him when he wasn't looking. She wanted to know what he was hiding from her down there. She made her way down the stairs to the room. No one else was down there. She was alone. She walked into the room and stood there for a moment and looked around. She was working up the courage to look in the closet. When she had finally mustarded up the courage she slowly walked over to the closet. Her shoes echoed on the cement floor. She reached for the knob, but then pulled her hand back.

She started to turn around and run. This is ridiculous she said to herself, there's probably nothing in there. She reached for the knob and turned it, she swung the door open. The stench almost knocked her over. But what she saw in the corner really freaked her out. She started to scream, but caught herself. She put her hand over her mouth and shut the door. She leaned against the door trying to catch her breath. Then she heard someone coming down the stairs. She looked for a place to hide. She looked around and saw some boxes in the corner; she ran over there and crouched down behind them. Skyler and another officer walked into the room. They stopped in the middle of the room. Skyler turned to the officer.

"I want you to make sure no one gets in here and messes with things," said Skyler.

"Yes, sir," said the officer.

"Make sure Ashlie doesn't open that door," said Skyler. "I don't know how she'd react to seeing her father like that."

"No problem," said the officer.

"I want to let her down easy," Skyler said.

They left the room. She could hear them going back up the stairs. She sat down against the wall. She could feel the dampness and cold from the cement wall on her back, but she didn't care. It was as if her world was crashing down around her. Her head started spinning. It seemed like a million questions were spinning around in her head like a giant whirlwind. She had to find her sister. She needed some answers.

Ashlie got up and walked out of the room. She quietly walked up the stairs. When she got to the top she slowly opened the door. She didn't see anyone, so stepped out and shut the door. Then she heard the front door open.

She hurried and ran into the kitchen. It was Skyler again. He headed for the basement door. He opened it and stuck his head in and called out for Ashlie. Ashlie hurried and ducked out the back door, she headed straight for her car. As she reached for the handle an officer called out to her. He said that Skyler was looking for her. She told him to tell Skyler that she was exhausted and was going home to rest and that she would see him first thing in the morning. He said he would give him the message. Ashlie hurried and got in her car. She started it up and put in reverse and sped out of there. She wanted to get out of there before Skyler spotted her. As she headed down the street she looked in her rearview mirror and saw Skyler jumping up and down and waving his hands. She pretended not to see him and kept going.

Skyler stomped back to the house. He was not happy about Ashlie leaving without him. He didn't want her being alone with her sister still running around. He chewed on the officer's butt for letting her go. The officer tried to explain to him that he thought that he just didn't want her in the house. Skyler just thru his hands up in the air and stomped off. Then he turned around and told the officer that he wanted him to go find her and keep an eye on her. Cause if any thing happened to her, he was in deep shit. The officer got in his car and sped off. It wasn't long and the forensic team was there. Skyler showed them where to go. He warned them about the smell.

CHAPTER 6

W HEN ASHLIE PULLED into the parking lot at her apartment building she turned off her car and just sat there. She looked down at the photo album and picked it up. She got out of her car and locked the doors. As she was heading toward the stairs she noticed a strange pickup there. It looked like someone was sitting in the driver's seat. She walked over to it she notice that it had state license plates on it and on the side of the door was forest ranger. I wonder if it's that guy that his wife reported missing she thought to herself. She knocked on his window but he didn't respond. She tried the door handle but it was locked. She decided to go up stairs to her apartment and call it in when someone grabbed her from behind. Ashlie struggled to get free. But they were strong. Then they whispered in her ear, "I see you finally made it little sister," Chills went up the back of Ashlie's neck.

"Dee? I was trying to find you," said Ashlie.

"Well here I am," said Dee.

"Look Dee I brought the album for us to look at," said Ashlie.

"That thing holds nothing but bad memories," she snarled, knocking it out of Ashlie's arms.

"Why don't we go up to my apartment and have a cup of coffee and look at it," said Ashlie, her voice shaking.

"I told you I'm not interested in looking at those stupid pictures," she said.

Dee pushed Ashlie towards the stairs kicking the album out of the way. Ashlie didn't understand why Dee was so full of hate.

"So I see you noticed my latest conquest," said Dee laughing.

"Another one, But why?" asked Ashlie.

"The guy was a jerk," said Dee.

"How do you know, you didn't even know him?" said Ashlie.

"Because he was no good," said Dee angrily. "He hurt his wife. But he won't be doing that anymore, will he? She laughed out loud."

"Is that why you killed daddy," said Ashlie.

"Oh, I see you found him," said Dee.

"But why, you said you loved him," said Ashlie.

"I'll tell you all about it when we get up stairs," she said, pushing Ashlie up the stairs.

Ashlie was hoping that Skyler didn't figure out where she was, at least not yet. She still believed she could help her sister. She just needed time.

Skyler was going out of his mind. He couldn't leave until everything was taken care of. The officer radioed in that he had lost Ashlie. He had never felt so helpless in his life. It seemed like they were taking forever. He knew he couldn't hurry them up. The captain would have his ass if he messed things up. He paced back and forth. He was snapping at everyone. The officers started avoiding him.

He was barking out orders like a mad dog. Finally one officer approached him and told him that he didn't think it was fair that he was jumping on everyone for no reason. Skyler said he was right and apologized to everyone. They said they understood. Skyler had a pretty good idea where Ashlie was. After he mad sure she was alright he was going to chew her butt out for leaving.

Ashlie had a plan and she hoped it worked. When they got to the top of the stairs Dee was winded. She told Ashlie she needed to find an apartment with no stairs. Ashlie didn't comment. She unlocked the door and pushed it open. Dee was right behind her. Ashlie looked around for something to hit Dee over the head with and knock her out. She figured once she was out she would tie her up and call for help. But Dee had plans of her own. She pushed Ashlie down on the couch and she sat across from her in an over stuffed chair. Then she started rambling on about how much she loved their father. How he would come to her every night after mother would fall asleep. Then one night as they made love she walked in on them. She was furious and sent him away. Ashlie started getting sick to her stomach. Then she went on to tell Ashlie how she would meet him at his apartment. But one day she went there and he had another woman with him. He told her that what they were doing was wrong and not to come back. The woman was his new wife. So she plotted to get him to come over and she killed him. Then she told Ashlie that she had killed their mother, not Ashlie. She blamed her for their father finding someone else. She told Ashlie that she convinced their father to make love to her one last time, and then she killed him. Ashlie couldn't believe her ears. All these years she carried around the guilt. And how scared she was when they locked her up in the nut house. When all along it was her sister that should have been locked up. She knew now she was beyond help. She was a fricking basket case. Now she wished she had stayed put, like Skyler told to do. You know after you've killed once then it's pretty easy Dee told Ashlie. Ashlie started to get up, but Dee told her to stay put. Dee got up and walked over to the phone and picked it up and brought it over to Ashlie. She told her to call Skyler and tell him to come over here. Ashlie tried to explain to her that he wasn't home, But Dee persisted. Ashlie dialed the station. She told the officer that picked up the phone, that if Skyler called in, to tell him that she is home and to come over. She thanked him and hung up. Five minutes later the phone rang, Dee picked it up. It was Skyler.

"Nice to hear your voice again," said Dee.

"Where's Ashlie?" asked Skyler.

Dee could hear the panic in his voice.

"Oh, she's fine," she answered.

"Let me talk to her!" he said raising his voice.

"Calm down here she is."

"Skyler, I'm okay," said Ashlie.

"Are you sure?" asked Skyler.

Dee jerked the phone out of Ashlie's hand.

"Now listen up, she's fine, and if you want her to stay that way I suggest you get over here pronto," said Dee.

Before Skyler could say any more Dee hung up the phone. Well that should get him over here fast.

"What do you want?" asked Ashlie.

"What I want is for you to suffer, just like I have," said Dee.

"Your not suffering, your just plan ass sick," said Ashlie.

"Don't use that tone of voice with me young lady," said Dee.

She got up and walked over to Ashlie and slapped her across the face.

"Who do you think you are hitting me!" yelled Ashlie.

"Who do you think I am, I'm your mother," she said.

"Our Mother is dead, you stupid bitch," yelled Ashlie.

Dee raised her hand up to hit Ashlie and Ashlie kicked her and sent her backwards over the coffee table. Ashlie jumped up and ran for the door. She didn't look back to see if Dee was behind her. She ran for her car. But she didn't have her keys. She took off running down the street. Then she remembered Skyler was coming over. Ashlie remembered her cell phone was in her car. She could call Skyler on it and tell him what was going on. She turned around to go back and get her phone. Then she stopped. I can't just run back, I need a plan. She thought to herself. She knew Dee would be waiting for her. It was dark on the other side of the street so she decided to sneak back that way. When she got back to the apartments she could see her apartment door was closed. I wonder where she is, Ashlie thought to herself. Ashlie stood there in the dark planning her next move when someone grabbed her from behind. Ashlie let out a scream. They put they're hand over her mouth and pulled her to the ground. She started kicking. Then she heard some yell ow. It was Skyler. He saw her run out of the apartment and down the road. He knew she would come back.

"You scared the crap out of me," said Ashlie.

"Sorry, but I didn't know what else to do," said Skyler. "I was about to go up to your apartment when I saw you run out."

"Is my sister still in there?" asked Ashlie.

"As far as I know," he said. "Back up is on the way. I think we should wait for them to get here."

"I'm with you on that one," she said. "My sister is worse off than I thought. You see that pick up over there; the guy in it is dead."

"Your sister's handy work?" said Skyler.

"Yep, I guess he pissed her off," said Ashlie.

"I hope they don't show up with they're sirens on, said Skyler.

Just as he finished his sentence sirens came blasting up the street.

"So much for the quiet approach," said Ashlie.

When the police cars got there Ashlie and Skyler crossed the street. Skyler told them to call the meat wagon. The guy in the truck is dead. With all the commotion going on Mrs. Day stuck her head out the door. Ashlie could hear her husband yelling at her to get back in and mind her own business. Ashlie told her to go back in and lock her door. She shut the door. Then Ashlie noticed her curtains pulled apart and her nose pressed against the window. Ashlie chuckled to herself. Skyler and Ashlie headed up the stairs to her apartment. When they got in there Dee was gone. She had scribbled across a mirror in Ashlie's living room it read, "CATCH ME IF YOU CAN." Skyler was at a loss. He paced back and forth. Not knowing what their next move would be. He was hoping that she wouldn't kill anymore. He knew she couldn't go back to her place and get her tools. He hoped she wasn't carrying a spare pare.

"So what are you thinking?" asked Ashlie.

"I'm hoping we catch your sister before she hurts anyone else," said Skyler.

"I hope so to," said Ashlie. "She's one sick puppy."

"You can say that again," said Skyler.

They went back out side. When they got down to the bottom of the stairs the captain was pulling up.

"Shit, that's all we need," said Skyler.

"What?" asked Ashlie.

"The captain just pulled up," said Skyler. "And he's gonna want some answers. And right now I'm all out of them."

They tried to avoid him; they turned around and started to walk up the stairs when he spotted them. He jumped out of his car and started yelling. They stopped and turned around.

"You two want to tell me what the hell is going on here?" he yelled.

"Can't we talk tomorrow?" said Ashlie. "It's been a long day."

"NO, we can't!" screamed the captain. "I want answers now!"

"Calm down, your going to have a heart attack," said Skyler.

"I'll calm down when you explain things to me," said the captain.

Ashlie rolled her eyes and sat down on the stairs. She knew it was going to be a long night and a lot of paper work. Skyler sat down beside her. The captain put his foot up on the first step and laid his arm across his knee. Skyler proceeded to tell him everything. He tried to remember every detail. Ashlie helped him fill in the blanks.

"So your telling me that you don't know were she is?" asked the captain.

"Basically, yea," answered Ashlie.

"Then why are you sitting here on your butts?" yelled the captain.

"Because you told us to stay and explain things to you," answered Skyler raising his voice.

"Well, we're done now, so get moving," he yelled.

They got up and went back up the stairs toward Ahslie's apartment.

"Were are you two going?" he demanded.

"We're going up stairs to look for clues," said Ashlie.

"Fine," said the captain.

He stomped off toward his car and got in and took off. They breathed a sign of relief. They went on up stairs. Ashlie thought maybe Dee might have left a clue to where she might go. They searched the whole apartment but couldn't find anything. They collapsed on the sofa.

"Are you hungry?" asked Ashlie.

"Yea, I'm starving," said Skyler.

"Why don't we go get something to eat," said Ashlie.

"Sounds like a great idea to me," said Skyler.

"Great, so what are you hungry for?" asked Ashlie.

"Anything but hotdogs," said Skyler.

Ashlie laughed. As she laughed Skyler thought to himself, she has a beautiful laugh. I want to spend the rest of my life listening to her laugh. He looked at her and smiled.

"What?" she asked.

"You're beautiful," he said.

"You need your eyes checked," she said laughing.

He leaned over and kissed her. He whispered in her ear, I love you. She smiled and kissed him back. They got up and headed out the door. Ashlie made sure the door was locked and she took the spare key with her. She didn't want to come back and have Dee waiting for her.

When Dee heard the door click shut she emerged out of the closet. So they want to know where I am, she said to herself. She walked over to the window and peeked thru the curtains. She watched as Skyler and Ashlie got in the car and backed out and headed down the street. I guess I'll just have to give them a few hints she said. She watched until the last police car left. She went into the kitchen and opened a drawer. She pulled out a meat cleaver and a butcher knife. These will work nice for my next job she said. Then she wrote across the counter top, "SORRY YOU MISSED ME," Your loving sister Dee. She laughed out loud as she headed for the door. She decided to go down the side stairs so the noisy neighbor below didn't see her.

Ashlie wasn't sure what she was hungry for, so they went to a restaurant that had a little bit of everything. She decided on the cheeseburger with fries. Skyler ordered the same. It wasn't long and their food came. Ashlie hurried and put her burger together and took a bite. It was like heaven in her mouth. She was starving. Skyler just sat there staring at her. She looked at him.

"What?" she asked.

"Boy you must be real hungry," he said.

"I am, I haven't eaten since breakfast," she said.

"No wonder you're hungry," he said. "So do you have any clues as to where your sister might have gone?"

"No, I wish I did," she said. "But I have a feeling that she will contact me sooner or later."

"Well I hope its sooner," he said.

"Me to," she said, shoving the piece of cheeseburger in her mouth.

Just as she swallowed the last bite the waitress came over and asked if they wanted dessert. Skyler said no, but Ashlie said yes. She ordered a piece of chocolate cake with ice cream. When the waitress brought it to the table Skyler said, "That looks pretty good." Ashlie offers to share it with him. He picked up his fork and took a bite. Not bad he said. He helped Ashlie finish off the cake and ice cream. The waitress asked if they wanted anything else. They said, "no" and she brought the check. Skyler paid for dinner. Ashlie left the tip. Ashlie felt better now that her stomach was full. She felt now that she could concentrate on the case. They walked out to the car and got in. They sat there for a few minutes talking about what to do next. She suggested that they go back to Dee's house to look around some more.

Maybe they could find a clue about where she likes to go. Skyler thought that was a good idea. He started up the car and headed towards Dee's house. Ashlie was little bit nervous about going back inside the house. Skyler could see it in her face. He pulled into the driveway of Dee's house. He turned off the car and turned to Ashlie and said, "If you don't feel right about this, we can come back tomorrow when its daylight." No, I'm okay she said. She liked the idea more when they were at the restaurant, than she did now. But she knew she couldn't back out now. They had to find Dee, before she killed again.

Dee put the knife in a small duffle bag she found in Ashlie's closet. She walked down the sidewalk toward town. She kept mumbling to herself. She was out of control. She had lost all sense of reality. She kept hearing voices in her head. She was a walking time bomb. She picked up the pace. She had a job to do and she wanted to finish it before it was time. She was almost to the point that she was jogging. When she got into town she was out of breath. She was standing at a corner trying to catch her breath when she heard a voice say, "are you okay miss?" It was a man in his late fifties. She turned to him and said, "thank god you're here, someone was chasing me," Then she asked him if he could walk her back to her hotel. He gladly obliged. She smiled. As they walked down the sidewalk she made a turn into an alley. He hesitated, and then she told him it was a short cut. When they got half way down the alley she came on to him. He didn't resist. She run her hand down his pants. He started ripping her shirt off and in an instant she grabbed one of the knives and plunged it into his chest. He dropped to the ground and she took his pants off and she carefully begins to cut off his testicles and then his penis. He gasps for one last breath and then dies. She shoves his cock into his mouth and walks off. She turns around and spits on him and then says, "Your nothing but a cock sucker." She laughs out loud and heads back onto the street.

When Ashlie walked thru the door in Dee's house she got goose bumps. This place gives me the creeps she told Skyler. He agreed with her. They made their way to the basement door. Skyler slowly opened it. They carefully went down the stairs. It seemed to Ashlie that it was colder than it was before down here. It was probably my imagination she thought to herself. When they got to the bottom of the stairs Skyler turned on the light. It swung back and forth casting shadows on the walls and in the corners. Ashlie jumped. She could have sworn she saw someone crouched down in the far corner of the room. She reached up and grabbed the light and shined it in the corner. Something scurried across the room. Ashlie screamed and made Skyler jump. He turned around and looked at her. She told him that she saw something. He told her it was probably a rat or a stray cat. But she wasn't convinced, it was too big. She stayed close to Skyler as they headed for the room. Ashlie felt as though someone was watching them.

Skyler and Ashlie searched the room for papers and anything else that might give them an idea of where Dee might have gone. Ashlie was looking in a desk and came across Dee's diary. She told Skyler that she found something.

He went over to Ashlie to see what she had found. They decided to take it and go back to Ashlie's place and read it.

Ashlie couldn't get out of there fast enough. She almost runs Skyler over getting up the stairs. He couldn't figure out what her hurry was. By the time Skyler got up the stairs Ashlie was already thru the door and headed for the front door. She must really want to read that diary he thought to himself. When he got out the front door Ashlie was sitting in the car waiting for him. He shut the door of the house and made sure it was locked and went to get in the car. As Skyler was getting in the car Ashlie saw someone in the window of the house. She started yelling at Skyler to look. But by the time he turned around they were gone. She swore up and down someone was looking out the window. He asked her if it would make her feel better if he went back in and checked. But she said no. Skyler backed out of the driveway and headed for Ashlie's Apartment.

Chapter 7

*D*EE MADE HER way back onto the street. She decided to look for a ride to take her back home. She needed to get back there. Little Damien needed her. She walked for several blocks before she found an older man to give her a ride. She got into his car and smiled at him. She asked him if he would give her ride to her house. She told him that her car had broken down and she needed to get home. He eyed her up and down and smiled and said sure get in. She knew what was on his mind and she had plans of her own. She asked him if he would like to go park before he took her home. He kind of hesitated, but changed his mind. He pulled over to the curb and turned off the car. She told him that an alley would be better, that way they wouldn't be disturbed. He started up the car and started driving until he came to an alley way, he quickly turned in. He turned off the car. Dee started unbuttoning her shirt. He was on her in a minute. He was ripping at her shirt. He started pulling at her pants. Before she knew it he was on her. As quick as he started he was done. He got off and put his clothes back on and told her to get out. She couldn't believe her ears. He thru twenty dollars at her and told her to take a hike. That pissed her off. She pulled out a knife and drove it into his chest. Then she jumped out of the car and ran to the driver's door and opened it. She dragged him out onto the ground. She pulled his pants down and took another knife and started craving up his privates. When she was done she jumped into the driver's seat of the car and sped away. She could hear him screaming in pain. She just laughed.

Skyler and Ashlie finally got back to Ashlie's apartment. Ashlie was exhausted. She convinced Skyler to go to bed and read the diary in the morning. Skyler didn't argue he was too tired. Ashlie thought maybe he would want to make love. She started kissing him; but he just turned over and went to sleep. Ashlie was now too upset to sleep. She tossed and turned but couldn't go to sleep. She got up and went into the living room to read the diary. Most of the beginning of it was about their childhood. Then she came up on the part about a child. Dee had given birth to a baby boy. She had him at home. Then Ashlie's stomach turned when she read the part about it being their father's child. Dee talked about it being a joyous time for her. The three of them living together. Then that all changed when he decided to leave. That was when she decided she had to stop him. He had been with them ever since. Ashlie just sat there staring. Then she remembered the person in the house. It must be the boy Ashlie thought to herself. Then she decided to go back to Dee's and try to find the boy. He must be at least 16 Ashlie thought to herself. Ashlie quietly slipped into the bedroom to get her clothes. Skyler was lying on his back snoring. She decided to get her clothes and get dressed in the living room. She hurried up and gathered up her clothes. She got dressed and quietly slipped out the door. She got in the car and started it up and headed down the street to Dee's house.

Dee pulled into the drive way of her house. She slammed the car into park and hurried up and jumped out and ran to the house. She tried opening the door but it was locked. She called out to Damien to let her in. The door lock clicked and Dee opened it. She hugged and kissed him and asked if he was okay. He nodded yes. She assured him that everything was going to be okay. She told him that he looked tired and need to go lay down. She took him by the hand and led him into her bed room and set him down on the bed. She took his shirt off and then started to take his pants off. He tried to push her away. Because he knew what she was going to do. He didn't want it any more. But she told him that if he wasn't nice that she would have to tie him up again. He gave in. He knew that if he didn't perform she would beat him and lock him up. Tears run down his face. She could see the tears in his eyes. She told him to be a man not a baby. He wanted to kill her right there and then. But he was scared to be alone. He had never been around anyone but her. So he just did as he was told.

When Ashlie got close to Dee's house she parked down the block. She didn't want to scare the boy. She walked up the sidewalk. She saw a car in Dee's driveway. She slowly walked up to it. It was running but no one was in it. She walked towards the house. She reached for the door handle and turned it, the door opened. She quietly walked in. She headed toward the basement when she felt a pain in her head. Then every thing went black. When she woke up she was on the bed tied up. Her clothes had been removed. She jerked her hands but they were tied up to tight.

"Welcome home," said Dee.

"What are you going to do to me?" asked Ashlie.

"Not me," said Dee. "Meet my son Damien. He's never seen another woman before. I think he's pretty excited."

"You're sick; I'm his Aunt for god's sake!" Ashlie said with fear in her voice.

"So, he's been screwing me since he was 10," she said laughing.

Dee motioned Damien to get on Ashlie. He stood there and hesitated. Dee pushed him on the bed. He crawled on top off Ashlie. Ashlie begged him not to do it. He put his finger over her mouth. Then he looked over at his mother, she had a big smile on her face. He jumped up and grabbed her and slammed her against the wall. He kept screaming at her saying, "No more! NO more!" He had her by the throat. She couldn't breath and started to loose consciousness. Ashlie kept yelling no Damien let go of her. When he finally let go she slid down the wall and sat down on the floor and coughed and gasped for air. Damien went over to the bed and untied Ashlie and wrapped a blanked around her. He went over to his mother and helped her up. He told Ashlie to leave. Ashlie didn't want to leave Damien there. He grabbed her by the arm and led her to the front door and opened it and pushed her out side and locked the door behind her. Ashlie yelled and pounded on the door but Damien just ignored her. He went and got his mother and took her down to the basement. He went back up to the kitchen and lit a candle, and then he turned on the gas to the stove and blew out the pilots. He went back to the basement and locked the basement door on the way down. He helped his mother up and took her to his room. He laid her down on the bed and lay down next to her. He wrapped his arms around her and kissed her. He told her he loved her and that he was sorry if he hurt her. She smiled and told it was okay. That they would be okay.

Ashlie ran around the house trying to open a window. She knew something was wrong. When she went past the kitchen window she noticed a candle burning on the stove. She knew right away what they were planning. She ran back to the front of the house. She looked around the door to see if there was a key. As she was looking around a bush she heard a loud explosion and she knew right away what happened. Before she could get on her feet the house exploded. The blast sent Ashlie hurdling across the front lawn. The house was engulfed in flames. She tried to get up but pain shot thru her body. All she could do was lay there and watch. It wasn't long and she could hear sirens coming up the street. People where gathering in the streets. Everything went black.

When Ashlie woke up Skyler was staring down at her.

"You got quite a jolt," he said.

"Where am I?" she asked.

"They brought you into the hospital last night," he said.

"What about Dee and Damien?" she asked.

Skyler got a puzzled look on his face.

"They were in the house when it exploded," she said.

"They didn't find any bodies," said Skyler.

"But they were in there!" said Ashlie raising her voice.

"You got quiet a nasty bump on you head, why don't you get some rest and well talk about this later," said Skyler.

"Are you hiding something from me?" she asked.

"No, why would I be hiding something from you," he said, a little annoyed.

When Skyler left the room Ashlie could see him whispering something to the nurse and the nurse nodded her head. I wonder what there up to Ashlie thought to herself. He should know I find out everything. Ashlie sat back in bed and stared at the ceiling. She decided to turn on the television to see if it made the news. When she turned it on it was just saying more on that explosion in a minute. After it seemed like fifteen commercials the news came back on. When it came back on it showed Dee's house totally engulfed in flames. They said no one was in the house and they didn't have the exact cause of the fire. How can that be said Ashlie to herself? I know they were in there. How could they have gotten out? Ashlie knew there bodies had to still be in there. If only she could get out of this bed. Ashlie was lost in thought when Skyler came back into her room. She looked up at him.

"They were in that house," said Ashlie.

"If they were in there we would have found some evidence of them," said Skyler.

"They must have got out some how," said Ashlie.

"There was no way they could have gotten out alive," said Skyler. "There was nothing left of the house.

"We need to go look," said Ashlie.

"They've already went over everything," he said.

"Well they must've have missed something," she said.

Ashlie started to get up, when Skyler stopped her.

"You're not going anywhere," he said.

"I need closure," she said.

"What you need right now is rest," said Skyler.

After some protesting and Skyler promising that they would check it out when she was feeling better, Ashlie laid back down. Ashlie hadn't realized how much Skyler really meant to her. She also realized that she didn't want to live without him.

Ashlie closed her eyes. Her thoughts went toward Damien and what his life must have been like living with a crazy mother. It was almost like dasivu. Was he her nephew or her brother? Will I ever hear from Dee again? She thought to herself. Ashlie opened her eyes and sat up in bed. Skyler looked at her.

"What if Dee tries to leave the country?" said Ashlie.

"We have the airports covered," said Skyler.

"But do they know to look for two people?" asked Ashlie.

"Airport security has been warned," said Skyler.

Ashlie had an uneasy feeling. She knew that her sister was resourceful. And knowing Dee she probably had an escape plan all along.

"Hey, mom you'd better hurry up, we're gonna miss our flight," said Damien.

"Okay, don't rush me," said Dee.

"So do you think your gonna like Italy?" asked Damien.

"I think it's gonna make a wonderful new start for the two of us," said Dee.

As they announced the flight number Dee and Damien head for the gate. They settled in their seats and waited for the plane to take off. Dee looked out the window and smiled. She turned to Damien and said," You know I'm going to miss Ashlie. I think she would have made you a nice wife. He looked at his mother and smiled. It wasn't long when the flight attendant told them to buckle up the plane was starting to take off. They held hands and set back in their seats and settled in for the long flight. Dee closed her eyes as the plane took off down the run way. She was looking forward to a new start.

The plane started to take off down the runway, when the pilot announced over the intercom that there was going to be a delay and that they were turning around. Dee looked at Damien and knew that it was over. He looked at his mother and saw tears running down her face. He held her hand tight and didn't say a word.

The plane came to a stop and the door opened. Dee took a deep breath and braced herself. She turned to Damien. He knew that this was the last time that he would see his mother.

"I'll always love you," she said to him.

"I know mom," he said.

She leaned over him and gave one last kiss. The police slowly made their way up the aisle. When they got to Dees seat they stopped.

"Dee Wilson, you're under arrest, for murder," said one of the officers.

She started to stand up, and then she put something in her mouth. She collapsed back into her seat.

"No!" screamed Damien.

The officers just stood there in shock. Damien grabbed a gun from one of the officers. He was waving it around screaming.

"Son give me the gun!" said the officer.

"No! You killed my mother," he said.

"Just hand over the gun so we can help her!" said the officer.

Damien put the gun in his mouth and pulled the trigger. But the gun jammed. One of the officers ran over and grabbed the gun out of his hand. They cuffed him. Damien dropped to the ground and cried. The other officers were trying to calm the rest of the plane down. They couldn't find any pulse on Dee. They picked him up and escorted him off the plane. He was screaming at the top of his lungs for his mom.

When Skyler got the news he didn't know how to break it to Ashlie. He figured he'd had better tell her before she heard it from some where else. When he walked into Ashlie's room she was asleep. He hated to wake her. She looked so peaceful. He walked over to her bed and leaned over and kissed her. She opened her eyes.

"Hey," she said.

"Hey, yourself," he said.

"Did they find Dee?" she asked.

He hung his head. He took his hand in hers. She knew that the news wasn't good. She braced herself.

"She was on a flight to Italy," he said.

"And?" she said.

"And she knew we had her, so she took something," he said, "there was nothing we could do to save her."

A tear rolled down Ashlie's face.

"What about Damien?" she asked.

"He going to be fine," said Skyler. "He grabbed a gun from one of the officers, but luckily it jammed."

Skyler wiped the tears from Ashlie's face. He held her close in his arms. He knew that even thought what Dee had done she was the only family that Ashlie thought she had. She never got to know her nephew. But she was hoping that would change. All those years of bitterness kept her and her sister apart.

Ashlie laid the flowers on Dee's grave. Skyler stood back and watched.

"I hope that she finally found peace," said Ashlie.

"I'm sure she has," said Skyler. But he wondered if someone that sick could ever find peace.

He put his arm around Ashlie.

"I think I finally will have some closure," she said.

"Come on lets go home," said Skyler.

That sounded real nice to Ashlie. She turned to Skyler and smiled. He leaned over and kissed her.

"You know what would be nice?" said Ashlie.

"Waking up next to each other every morning," he said.

"Yea, I think I would love that," she said.

Ashlie stopped and turned around and took one last look at the graves. I guess if hadn't been for my sister Skyler and I wouldn't be together she thought to herself. I wonder if she realizes that. Ashlie turned and around and they walked hand in hand back to the car. I hope now she has found peace Ashlie thought to herself. She couldn't even imagine the torment that was going on in her mind. She thought turned back to her nephew and what Dee had put him through.

"So what do you think is going to happen to Damien?" asked Ashlie.

"He'll be in an institution," said Skyler, "He's going to need a lot of help,"

"How long do think he'll be there?" she asked.

"Not sure," said Skyler.

"I'd like to see him," said Ashlie.

"I don't think that's a good idea, right now," said Skyler, "He's a pretty angry kid right now."

"I can understand why," she said. "His mother was his world and now she's gone."

CHAPTER 8

*D*AMIEN SAT THERE staring at the wall clutching a picture of his mother in his hand.

"Damien can you tell me how your feeling," asked Dr. Whyte.

"How the hell do you think I feel!" yelled Damien. "My mother is dead!"

"How does that make you feel?" asked the Dr.

"Are fricking kidding me!" says Damien. "What are you and idiot, and your suppose to have the education!"

"I'm just trying to help," said the Dr.

"You can help by leaving me alone," said Damien.

"I can't do that," said the Dr. "I just trying to do my job."

"I want to be a lone," said Damien.

The doctor held out his hand. Damien looked at him confused. Then he pointed to his hand with the picture. Damien pulled to toward his chest. But the doctor was persistent. But so was Damien. The Doctor moved toward Damien. Damien got up and backed away.

"You can have it back, when you cooperate with us," said the Dr.

"If you want it come and get it," said Damien.

The Doctor nodded and before Damien could react two orderlies grabbed him by the arms and the doctor stuck him with a needle. Damien tried to resist but it was no use. He slumped to the floor. The doctor walked over and opened up his hand and took the picture. He leaned over and whispered in Damien's ear, "You can have this back, when you're a good boy. He told the orderlies to take him back to his room. They put him in a wheel chair and wheeled him down the hall to his room.

When Damien woke up he was in his room. He looked down at his hand. His momma's picture was gone. He slammed his fist against the wall. Why did you leave me? He yelled and he beat his fist against the wall. The patient in the room next to him started yelling and beating on the wall. The door flew open to Damien room and the Doctor and orderly came in. The Doctor had a needle in his hand. Damien knew what that meant. He stopped hitting the wall. He begged him not to sedate him. He promised not to do it again. But all the begging didn't help. He plunged the needle into Damien's arm he let out a scream; then went limp. The doctor told the orderly to strap him down. He wasn't going to have some spoilt brat disrupting his hospital. The other patient in the next room was still yelling and banging on the wall. He told him when he was done there he wanted him to help him with patient in the next room.

Ashlie couldn't get Damien out of her mind. She felt that he needed her now that his mother was gone. She was the only family he had. Skyler told her that he would take her to see Damien when the time is right. She didn't like that answer. She had to see him. She didn't need Skyler to take her. She was a big girl. She could drive herself, she thought, and that's exactly what I'm going to do. She decided to make up an excuse as to why she couldn't go to work tomorrow. She'll Skyler to go with out her and she would meet him later. By the time he figures it out she'll be at the institution talking to Damien.

When Damien woke he was strapped to the bed. It brought back memories of what his mother use to do to him. He started yelling. A nurse came in.

"You need to keep it down," she said, "you disturbing the other patients."

"Untie me!" he said through tears.

"I wish I could," she said, "but only the doctor can give the orders to unstrap you."

"I'll be good, I promise," he said.

"Listen kid," she said, "Let me give you a little advice, be nice and follow the rules; things will be a lot easier on you, understand."

Damien nodded his head. He was puzzled why was she being so nice. There's got to be a catch he thought to himself. She must want something of me. He had trust issues, because of his mother. She would say one thing and do another. He couldn't trust her. She said she preparing for life. All women were that way. He closed his eyes and drifted off to sleep. He kept waking up hoping that the straps were gone. He started thinking about Ashlie. This is her fault, he thought. If it wasn't for her he and his mother would be far away together. He decided to make it his mission to pay her back for what he believed she did to his family. He laid out his plan in his mind. He smiled as he thought about it. The first thing is to get out of this place. When he woke up it was morning. The straps were gone. He sat up in bed and looked around. He was hungry. Just as he was wondering when breakfast was the door opened to his room. An orderly walked in. Damien looked him up and down. He was a large man. His head was shaved. He had on white pants and a white shirt. When Damien looked down at his shoes he thought that it was odd that they were red tennis shoes. He thought they should be white to match his clothes. His name tag read, Kyle. He didn't look like a Kyle thought Damien.

"Are you going to come eat breakfast?" said Kyle.

Damien got up and walked over to the door. Kyle let Damien go first. He followed behind him. Everyone walked to the cafeteria like cattle being drive by the cow dogs. They picked up their trays and went down the line. Damien picked up his tray and pushed it along. They didn't ask what you wanted; they just put stuff on your tray. Damien picked up his tray full of food and sat down at a table next to a girl. She had long blonde hair. It covered part of her face. It was hard to tell what she looked like. With giving it a second thought, Damien reached and pushed her hair out of her face. She cried and cowered down on the floor. Kyle came running over there. He grabbed Damien by the arm and jerked him up out of his seat. He didn't know he did anything wrong.

"Keep your hands to yourself," growled Kyle.

"Sorry I didn't know I did anything wrong," said Damien. "I just wanted to see her face.

"The rules are, you don't touch no one," said Kyle!

"I understand," said Damien.

Kyle let go of Damien's arm. He sat there quietly eating his breakfast. I have to get out of here, he thought.

When he was done Kyle walked back to his room.

"Are we allowed to have visitors?" asked Damien.

"You have to earn that privilege," said Kyle.

"How do you do that," asked Damien.

"By following the rules," said Kyle.

"Thanks," said Damien.

"By the way, sorry about your arm," said Kyle

"I understand," said Damien.

Kyle closed the door. Damien felt a cold chill go up his back when the key clicked in the lock. He remembers when his mother use to lock him in his room when he disobeyed. If I ever get out of here, I never going to be locked up again, he said to himself.

Ashlie was trying to figure out a way to get Skyler out of the apartment; without him getting suspicious. It was hard to do. But she finally convinced him to meet her at work. She was going to call the institution but remembered that her phone had been tapped. She figured it was safe on her cell phone.

"Lighthouse institution, how may I help you," said the woman on the phone.

"Yes I was calling enquire on a patient," said Ashlie.

"Are you a family member?" asked the woman.

"Yes I am," said Ashlie.

"What's the name?" asked the woman.

"Damien," said Ashlie.

"What's the last name? She asked.

"Wilson," answered Ashlie.

"I'm sorry, he isn't allowed visitors yet," she said.

"But I'm his Aunt," she said.

"Not even for a few minutes," begged Ashlie.

"I'm sorry Madame," she said. "He hasn't earned that privilege yet."

"Thank you for your time," said Ashlie. She hung up the phone. Madame? That makes feel old, she said to herself.

Ashlie thought about just showing up and flashing her badge. But she decided it wasn't worth risking her job.

Skyler was wondering where Ashlie was. I hope she ain't planning to do something crazy he mumbled to himself. He was lost in thought when the phone rang. Maybe that's here he thought. He picks up the receiver.

"Hello," said Skyler.

"Yea boss, it's me."

"Hey, Kyle, how's it going?" asked Skyler. "How's the boy doing?"

"So far not bad," he said.

"But I think we need to keep an eye on that doctor," he said. "He's pretty loose with the sedatives."

"I'll do a check on the good doctor," said Skyler.

"Okay, let me know what you find," said Kyle. "I gotta go."

"Okay, watch your back," said Skyler.

Just as Skyler hung up the phone Ashlie walked into the station.

"I was beginning to think you weren't coming in," said Skyler.

"I had some errands to run," said Ashlie.

"Did you get them done?" he asked.

"What?" asked Ashlie.

"Your errands," said Skyler. "Are you okay?"

"Yea, I'm fine, just tired," she said.

Skyler looked at like he knew she was hiding something. Ashlie just ignored him and sat down at her desk. She picked up a file and opened it. She pretended to read it. Skyler knew she was up to something, she was avoiding eye contact. He got up and walked behind.

"I didn't know you could read upside down," said Skyler.

"I can't," said Ashlie; flipping the file right side up. "Why are you standing over me anyway?"

"You might as well tell me what your up to, I'm going to find out anyway," he said.

"If I did, then you wouldn't have any thing to do, now would you?" she said; smiling.

"That's why I love you," he said.

"I know," she said. She knew she couldn't stay mad at Skyler long. She also knew that she would tell him about her phone call. But for now she would let him stew a while.

"How about we go get some lunch?" asked Skyler.

"I would like that," said Ashlie.

Damien sat there staring at the pictures on the wall. He was lost in thought when the doctor asked him a question. The doctor repeated himself, then cleared his throat. Damien looked at the doctor.

"What?" asked Damien?

"I said, that your Aunt called, how do you feel about that?" said the doctor.

Damien started to feel angry, but remembered what he was told.

"I'm not sure, I really don't know her," answered Damien. "I only met her once."

"Didn't your mother talk about her?" asked the doctor.

"I'd rather not talk about my mother right now," said Damien.

"What would you rather talk about," said the doctor.

"I really don't feel like talking about anything right now," said Damien.

"If you wish," said the doctor. "But remember the less cooperative you are the longer you will be here. You may go now."

If that's how they play the game I guess I can go along with it Damien thought to himself.

"No I'd like to talk," said Damien. "Maybe it will make me feel better."

"That's more like it," said the doctor smiling.

Damien wanted to grab the doctor and rip that smile off his face. He came across as an arrogant bastard. Damien hid anger toward Ashlie. He knew that if they thought he was a danger he would never get out of here. He decided he would kiss their butts and tell them what they want. That's how he got around his mother.

"So what do you want to know doc?" asked Damien.

The doctor smiled and leaned back in his chair. This is going to be so easy, thought Damien to himself. The doctor took notes and Damien told him what he wanted to hear. When they were done the doctor patted Damien on the back and told how good he had done. Damien smiled as Kyle escorted him back to his room.

"So how did it go?" asked Kyle?

"Good," said Damien. "I feel much better."

"That's great," said Kyle. "Keep it up and you'll get to spend time in the rec room. I'll see you at dinner time."

"Okay, thanks," said Damien.

Ashlie sat quietly eating her lunch. She had a lot on her mind. It kept wondering back to Damien. She felt sorry for him. He was just a kid. Her sister took his innocence away from him. She wondered if that was going to make him a bitter person. She had to admit that she wasn't going to miss her. She was an evil vindictive person.

"So what you thinking?" asked Skyler.

"I was thinking about Damien," she said. "Do you think he'll ever get out of there?"

"I'm not sure," said Skyler. "He's pretty messed up."

"I'd like to get to know him," she said.

"I think you should give it time," said Skyler. "Let him come to you."

"Maybe," said Ashlie.

"I think you should listen to me this time, I know what I'm talking about," said Skyler.

Ashlie tried to ignore Skyler. She didn't want to here it. She stared out the diner window. Skyler knew she wasn't listening. He knew he was wasting his breath. He decided to put a tail on her to make sure she didn't try anything stupid. He'd seen that look on her face before. The waitress laid the check on the table. Skyler picked it up. He paid the cashier and they walked back to the car. He opened the door for Ashlie and she got in. Just as he closed her door his phone rang. It was Kyle. Skyler didn't want Ashlie to know what was going on.

"What's up Kyle?" asked Skyler, "got to make it quick, Ashlie is here."

"The boy seems to be settling in okay," said Kyle. "I'm not sure if he is just playing along to get out of here or if he is sincere."

"Thanks, keep me posted," said Skyler.

"Sure thing," said Kyle.

Skyler hung up and got in the car. He could tell Ashlie was going ask about the phone call. He was surprised when she didn't say anything. Ashlie stared out the window as they drove back to the station. She was thinking about what Skyler said to her. Maybe he's right, she thought to herself. Maybe I'll let Damien come to me. Maybe he doesn't want anything to do with me. He probably blames me for his mothers death. She turned her back towards Skyler. She put her hand on his knee. He put his hand on hers and they smiled at each other. He pulled into the parking lot at the police station. He parked the car and turned off the key. He turned to Ashlie.

He blurted out, "will you marry me."

Before Ashlie could answer, he slipped a ring on her finger. She thought it would more Romantic. She to surprised to say anything. Skyler sat there staring at her waiting for an answer. Then he started worrying that she was going to say no. Ashlie sat there staring at the ring. Tear were rolling down her cheeks.

"Yes, I will," She said thru tears.

Skyler through his arms around her.

"You don't know how happy you made me," he said.

"Oh my gosh, I have a wedding to plan," she said.

They got out of the car and walked hand in hand to the station. They walked in the door with smiles on there faces. The captain wanted to know what they were so happy about. Ashlie showed him the ring. Well that's all fine and dandy he said. But we have work to do. Seems as though there was an escape at the mental institute. I need you two to check it out. One person dead a couple wounded. Skyler was surprised. He just talked to Kyle. He dialed Kyle's number.

"Hello," said Kyle.

"What's going on!" asked Skyler.

"It's the kid, he stabbed the doctor and took his keys," said Kyle. "I tried to stop him, he was like an animal."

"Are you okay?" asked Skyler.

"Yea, I'll be fine, but the doctor wasn't so lucky," said Kyle. "He stabbed him in the neck.

"He must've learned his knife skills from his mother," said Skyler.

"Listen, I think he's coming after Ashlie," said Kyle.

"Thanks for the heads up," said Skyler.

"Sure no problem," said Kyle. "By the way when you catch the little bastard, put a bullet in him for me."

Skyler hung up the phone and turned to Ashlie.

"What's going on?" she asked.

"It's Damien, he's escaped, and coming after you," he said.

"Are you sure?" asked Ashlie.

"We need to get you in a safe place," said Skyler.

"I'm not running," she said. "If he wants me, then bring it on."

"He's a very sick and angry boy," said Skyler. "He doesn't want a family reunion. He wants to kill you.

"I understand that," she said. "I scored high in the marksman class."

"I don't think you'll be able to pull the trigger," said Skyler.

Ashlie was about to argue with Skyler when a blue car come speeding into the parking lot. It was headed straight for them. Ashlie's eye got big. She could move. All she could do was point. Skyler turned around to see the car coming at them. He grabbed Ashlie and picked her up and threw her over his shoulder and ran toward the station. He heard a loud crash and then an explosion. He turned around to see both cars engulfed in flames. He put Ashlie down.

"You sure pick a bad time to be speechless," said Skyler.

Ashlie just stood there. Finally she spoke.

"I can't believe what just happened," she said.

"I told you Damien was angry," said Skyler.

"I won't believe he was in that car until I see the autopsy report," said Ashlie.

"That Kid is resourceful."

"You think he would stage his own death?" asked Skyler.

"I know he would," said Ashlie.

Ashlie could hear the sirens from the fire trucks coming. She wondered who was in the car. If that wasn't Damien in car, would he come after her or disappear. She got goosebumps thinking about. Would she spend the rest of her life looking over her shoulder and sleeping with a gun under pillow? I'm not going to be a victim she thought to herself. He's not going to steal my happiness. I guess I'll just have to hunt him down.

"You were right, Ashlie," said Skyler. "That's not Damien, the body is too big."

"Well you know what I have to do," she said.

"We are in this together," said Skyler.

"I know," she said. Ashlie's phone rang.

"Hello," she said.

"Hi, Auntie," said Damien.

"What do you want?' asked Ashlie. "You know I'm going to hunt you down."

"Let the games begin," said Damien laughing.

Ashlie hung up.

"He won't be laughing when a put a bullet between his eyes," said Ashlie.

"I think we have some vacation coming," said Skyler, "how about we go hunting.

"Sounds good to me," said Ashlie.

Ashlie was hoping that he would just go far away and leave her alone. But he was too much like his mother. She knew that the only way he would leave her alone is if she stopped him in his tracks. She didn't know how long or how far she would have to go but she had to do it. The wedding have to be put on hold until this job was done.

"Are you ready to go?" asked Skyler.

"Ready when you are," answered Ashlie.

"I guess we'll have to take your car, mine has mechanical problems," he said laughing.

"Yea, it over heated," she said chuckling.

They walked across the parking lot to Ashlie's car.

"Do you think the captain will miss us?" asked Ashlie.

"Maybe just a little bit," said Sklyer.

About the Author

I live in a small town in Nevada. We have a small farm. That keeps me busy. Besides writing I also enjoy being with my family. I come from a family of artist. I love animals. I have a varitity of them.